jess
by Mary Casanova

★ American Girl®

SCHOLASTIC INC.

For Tamara, with love and admiration

And with gratitude to Patrick Warrior, superb eco-guide,
for showing me the jungles of Belize,
and to Charlie, my husband and traveling companion,
for lending me a little extra courage when I needed it

ISBN 978-0-545-83742-2

12 11 10 9 8 7 6 5 4 3 2 1   15 16 17 18 19 20/0

Printed in the U.S.A.   40

First Scholastic printing, January 2015

Illustrations by Robert Papp

Contents

1

Good-bye, Home; Hello, Jungle

The plane rode air currents up and down and then dipped its wing, as if to point out the river that snaked below. My insides fluttered with excitement and I clutched the passport holder around my neck. For months I had waited, and now we were finally flying over Belize. The ocean stretched in one direction and, in the other, vast patches of green reached inland as far as I could see. "Mom, look! That must be the jungle!"

She leaned closer to look through my window, her sleek black hair tickling my cheek. "And just think, Jess," she said, "within that jungle are ruins, sacred caves, *cenotes*—huge water holes—and artifacts."

From his aisle seat, Dad chimed in. "So much yet to discover!" His sandy curls and fair skin made him a sure bet for sunburn the moment we landed. "Most of the Maya sites are still buried under hundreds of years of soil and trees. So many undiscovered sites . . . so many untold mysteries."

"Mysteries," I said, liking the sound of that word. An adventurous, intriguing word. But the actual work at an archeological dig site—squatting in a pit or sitting at a table, brushing away sand and dust from pieces of pottery or bone—was a bit slow for me.

"Oh, the mysteries of buried history!" Mom said, probably hoping I was showing genuine interest at last. "The artifacts we find give us a glimpse into the past. Once they're uncovered, they need to be studied and protected. But some people see them only as 'treasures' to be stolen and sold for profit. In fact, there's been a lot of talk about looters becoming bolder in Belize."

"And that's such a shame," Dad said. "Artifacts are keys to understanding the past and should be available to everyone to see and learn from."

I studied my parents. Two people couldn't look more different. Mom's great-grandparents came from Kyoto, Japan; Dad's grandparents were from Ireland and Scotland. But no matter how different Mom and Dad appeared, they shared one thing: they were both crazy about archeology. I had gone with them on other, smaller digs with some of their students, but their conservation work had never taken both of them—or me!—out of the States before.

"What about Caracol?" I asked. "Is looting a big problem there?" I wanted to show them that I'd been listening to their discussions over the past year. They hadn't planned to take any of us kids out of school for this trip, but I had convinced them to bring me along. For once, I wouldn't have my older brother and sister along to boss me around. On past trips they'd always hounded me to be careful. Well, maybe I had needed watching when I was little, but not anymore. This was the trip to prove I wasn't the "baby of the family" anymore—that I, Jess Akiko McConnell, was ten.

Dad shrugged and said, "Only a small portion of the Caracol ruins have been unearthed so far, and those have been protected. The rest are thought to stretch for some thirty miles, so we may never know what artifacts looters may have already found and taken."

As Mom and Dad leaned into one another, talking about their work, I stared out the window and tuned them out. If they had talked about soccer and how to score on a tough goalie, maybe I'd have paid better attention. But how could I? My stomach danced with jitters. I started making a mental list of "firsts" on this trip:

* *First trip out of the country*
* *First passport*
* *First time being home-schooled*
    (at least from January until May)
* *First time in the jungle*
* *First trip without my older brother and sister*

I nearly forgot! I unzipped my passport holder. Inside my passport I'd tucked two small folded notes. "Don't open these until the wheels of the plane touch down in Belize," Heather had said at the Houghton airport. "You promise?"

"Promise."

Heather and Jason were 16 and 17, and they were staying home so that they wouldn't miss out on their high school stuff. Grandma Emi was staying with them and she was a hawk about schoolwork, so Mom and Dad had felt okay about leaving them at home. "To do well," Grandma Emi was fond of saying, "you must study, study, study." I thought it was about time that someone watched *their* every move for a change.

The landing gear clunked and the plane tipped down. I peered out the window to watch. I loved the moment when the ground rushes up to greet the plane. Beyond the runway, fields and palm trees hurtled past, growing larger. Then, with a bounce, the plane settled on its wheels. Wing flaps dropped down outside my window. The engines roared, announcing our arrival as we rolled along.

I quickly unfolded the notes. The first one was written in my sister's perfect cursive:

Dear Jess,

I'll miss you while you're away, but have a great time with Mom and Dad. And don't forget: watch where you're walking. (Remember the rattler you almost stepped on in Montana? Well there are things worse than that where you're going.) But have fun!!! And don't forget your big sister!

Hugs and Butterflies,
Heather

I smiled to myself. "Butterflies" was our code word for kisses. When I was about four, Heather had taught me how to make butterfly kisses on her cheek with my eyelashes. But did she have to remind me about the rattler? That happened when I was a first-grader, when I hadn't known to look behind every single rock. The rattler had sprung, but luckily it hadn't bitten me.

The second note was on wrinkled paper and was printed so hard in pencil that some of the letters nearly went all the way through:

Hey Loppy

Don't do anything stupid okay?
Just kidding. But seriously, watch
out for those spiders and snakes
and crocodiles and things that
go bump in the night. We don't
want anything to happen to the
baby of the family.
Have a good time and don't do
anything I wouldn't do! Ha! I
might even miss you.

Your handsome and
wonderful brother,

Jason

Usually I hated when he called me "Loppy," the
nickname I'd earned as a toddler when I'd tried to call
a dog "puppy" but it hadn't come out right. Ever since,
that's what Jason called me, and the more I complained
that it sounded babyish, the more he loved to say it.

As the plane came to a stop, I tucked the notes
away and grabbed my backpack and Toshi, my toy
monkey. I stood up, stretched, and then stepped into the
aisle with a skip. We were here, and there would be no
more teasing or nagging for five whole months!

As I stepped down the landing stairway to the tarmac, a wall of scorching air hit me, nothing like the icy air and drifts of snow we'd left in Michigan. The heat nearly turned me to pudding. I squinted in the intense sunlight and followed my parents as we were swept into a low, green building and swallowed into one of several lines. Before long, a stern immigration agent stamped my passport, making it official—*I really was in Belize.*

We found our luggage and caught a rusty cab to the Belize City bus station. Along the way, we passed more palm trees, houses on stilts—some half-built and seemingly abandoned, a boy carrying bulging plastic bags, bony dogs that looked as if they were rarely fed, and horses tethered in roadside ditches. All in bright, bright sunlight. This was definitely *not* Houghton, Michigan.

Inside the crowded bus station, we waited in a line for tickets. I stood on tiptoe to look around. People were crammed like crayons in an old crayon box. Some were bright, fresh, and colorful, while others looked tired, as if worn down to drab stubs. In another line, a toothless man carried two baskets with live, colorful chickens. I wondered if they were his pets or on their way to market.

As I stood behind my parents, someone tap-tapped my shoulder. At first I thought it was Dad, somehow playing a joke on me. When I spun around, I came face-to-face with a boy shorter than me, his cheeks smudged, his clothes like well-used rags.

"Please, lady, can you spare a dollar?"

He was no more than eight or nine. And begging. I didn't know what to say. "I . . . um, uh . . . "

I looked to Mom and Dad, but their backs were turned. No one had told me how to handle this. I turned away and quickly tucked my passport holder inside my shirt—already I'd forgotten to keep it hidden from view! Hot and thick, the air pressed in around me. I wiped sweat from my forehead.

The boy tapped my shoulder again. "Please, lady—"

"I . . . I'm not a lady," I said, facing him and leaning back into my parents.

The boy pivoted and silently vanished into the crowd. After he disappeared, I relaxed a bit and thought about how lucky I was that I'd never had to beg. My family and I had always had everything we needed. I tried to imagine what it must be like not to.

People started yelling and someone bumped into me—hard! A mother with a toddler turned and wagged her finger at the teenage boys in line behind her. She scolded them in rapid Spanish—and then turned and with a smile said something to me. I didn't understand a word of it.

Mom and Dad glanced back, but they didn't seem overly worried, so I said nothing. I timidly smiled back at the lady, then looked around nervously for the boy. If he came back again, should I give him a dollar?

Suddenly I didn't feel so brave and adventurous. I wished that Jason were there to hoist me up on his big shoulders. I wanted the comfort of Heather's hand. On past trips, had I only *borrowed* my courage from them?

Mom and Dad turned away from the ticket window. Feeling more like three than ten, I grabbed Mom's hand and pulled my rolling suitcase behind me.

Dad held up our tickets and beamed. "This is going to be one big adventure. Are you ready, Jess?"

"Sure," I said, forcing a smile. I really *had* been ready, but now I wasn't so sure. I knew that once my parents got lost in their work at the dig, as they always did, I was going to have to figure out everything on my own—without Heather and Jason.

With a deep breath, I adjusted my backpack and held my head high—ready or not—and stepped outside to board the bus.

2

Ancient Ruins

The bus to San Ignacio was hot and crowded. People had to stand in the aisles, including the man with the chickens. The two-lane highway was dotted with hitchhikers of all ages. Rust-bucket pickups overflowed with riders in back. Beside a cantaloupe stand, a man sat in a horse-drawn buggy. His wide-brimmed straw hat shaded his pale skin and blond beard.

"Weird," I said as the bus drove on. "He looked Amish. Are there Amish people in Belize?"

"Amish or Mennonite," Dad said. "Originally the Mennonites came from the Netherlands and started settling here about fifty years ago."

"Do they speak Dutch then, or English?"

"No, sweetie. German."

"But I thought you said that *English* was the language here. And Spanish."

"Officially, yes. But Belize is a country of many languages."

Before long, we entered another city and pulled in at another bus station. Dad squeezed my hand a few times as we climbed down the steps.

A short man with bronze skin approached us. "The McConnells?" he asked.

"That's us," Dad said.

The man took off his Red Sox cap, held it to his sweat-dampened shirt, and extended his other hand. "Welcome! Welcome to the best place on earth!" he said, shaking my parents' hands. "I'm Michael Bol." Then he shook my hand. Creases played at the corners of his eyes and he seemed like an overgrown, mischief-making kid, yet he was probably my dad's age.

"And what's your name, young lady?"

"Jess," I said.

"Miss Jess, is this your first trip to Belize? And what do you think?"

I glanced around in the brilliant sunlight, trying to take it all in. Pastel-colored buildings lined narrow streets. People milled about stands filled with jewelry, carvings, brilliant fabrics, trinkets, and vegetables and fruits. Three schoolchildren in white and green uniforms skipped along. A girl about Heather's age buzzed by on a moped, her floral skirt pressed against her knees.

"Jess?" Mom asked. "Honey, did you hear Mr. Bol's question?"

"Oh—sorry." I didn't really know yet what I thought.

I was too caught up in all the new sights, sounds, and smells. And then there was the heat.

"I . . . I, um—I think it's great!"

"And it's your first trip?" he asked again. He must have thought I was totally spaced out.

"Uh-huh."

"Well, in Belize, we say, 'Expect the unexpected.' If you can remember that, Miss Jess, you'll be just fine. You're going to have such a great time here, you'll never want to go back home to Minnesota again."

"Michigan," I said politely. "We're from Michigan."

"Minnesota, Michigan, Montana . . . it's all snow to me," he said with a laugh. His laugh was the kind that reached your own belly and made you want to laugh along with him. "I went north one summer—and that was winter enough for me!" He laughed again as he and Dad packed our bags and gear in the back of his dusty, dented Jeep. Dad climbed into the front passenger seat, because he sometimes gets carsick. After Mom and I hopped in back and got settled in, Mr. Bol slid behind the wheel, started the engine, and took off. He popped in a CD, and bright music blared with a beat to match the bumpy road.

With the windows down, heat and dust billowed in. The breeze did little to cool my face. "Mr. Bol," I asked as politely as I could, "do you think you could turn on the air-conditioning, please?"

"Oh, it's on, Miss Jess." He glanced at me in the rearview mirror. "Long as we keep our windows open." He laughed. "We call this 'natural' air-conditioning."

"Oh," I said, embarrassed not to have realized that there was no air-conditioning.

Mom winked at me and then gathered her long and flying hair into a ponytail. I lifted my braids for a moment, which helped cool me a little.

We curved along roads with ruts deep enough to swallow our tires, roads with trucks stuck sideways, and even roads flooded by small rivers. But nothing stopped Mr. Bol. He talked on, one arm out the window, one arm draped over the top of the wheel. "Oh sure. I've worked with lots of archeologists, ornithologists, and geologists. Anyone who needs to get around Belize."

We dipped beneath a canopy of treetops so dense that the sun couldn't get through, and then climbed to the top of pine-covered slopes that almost reminded me of home.

I glanced at Dad, who was turning a little pale, but Mr. Bol didn't seem to notice. He just kept on talking. "Sure, I've been working with the Caracol teams for years. Lots of changes there recently. Just wait till you see the new road leading there."

"Really?" Mom asked, her ponytail bobbing as we bounced around potholes.

I clung with one hand to the safety handle above my door.

Dad glanced at Mr. Bol. "You're joking, right?"

"No," Mr. Bol continued. "Caracol is what you might call a national treasure, and we need a road to handle all the future tourists."

The drive was long, and in the heat I dozed off. Soon after I woke up, road crews appeared out of nowhere. Then the bumpy dirt road gave way to smooth asphalt.

Mr. Bol pointed to a distant green hill crowned in white. "That's it! That's Caracol!"

Mom and Dad grinned at each other.

Several miles later, we slowed to a stop at a huge parking lot, next to a thatched roof covering a dozen picnic tables. We were at the entrance to the Caracol ruins. With my head halfway out the window, I took a deep breath of steamy jungle air. I couldn't believe I was actually there.

"Come on, Miss Jess," Mr. Bol said from outside the Jeep. He waved me toward an official-looking brick building. "This isn't McDonald's—no drive-through.

Come in and introduce yourself to the staff and to Fuzz."

Fuzz? I climbed out of the Jeep and followed Mom and Dad into the brick building, which turned out to be the visitor center and ranger station. Inside, three uniformed men and one woman greeted us warmly.

A little black monkey with white markings was sitting on a table in front of the young uniformed woman. "Hi, I'm Barbara," she said. Then turning her head toward her companion, she added, "And this is Fuzz—short for 'Little Fuzzball.' She's a spider monkey and is the one who's *really* in charge here."

Fuzz held out her tiny hand toward me. She was a real, live version of my Toshi, only bigger—and brown instead of green!

"Does she want something?" I asked.

"Oh, she'll take fruits and nuts anytime from anyone, but we ask that people put her food down and then step away and let her eat."

"Why? Is she dangerous?"

"It's better for her, and for us. Go ahead, let her hold your finger. Just wash your hands after."

I extended my pinky finger and, sure enough, Fuzz grabbed it in her warm little hand and looked me straight in the eyes—almost like a person.

Barbara smiled. "Looks like she likes you."

"Is she yours?"

"Fuzz belongs to everyone here. Her parents were shot by poachers who planned to sell her illegally as a pet. She's been here three years and is free to leave whenever she wants. But after being bottle-fed and raised by humans, she thinks that she's a person, too."

Fuzz let go of my finger, leaped from Barbara's table to the floor, and then sat at my feet. With her little black eyes, she peered up at me and cocked her head.

"What?" I asked her.

"That's her way of saying 'Let's be friends.'" said Barbara. I extended my pinky finger again and Fuzz squeezed it, almost like a tiny handshake. With a grin, I turned to Mom and Dad, who couldn't have looked happier.

"We'll drive the Jeep ahead," Mr. Bol said, "and if you want to follow on foot, I bet your little friend there might come along."

I washed my hands in the rest room, and then walked behind the Jeep on the dirt road to the archeology camp. Fuzz skittered on all fours beside me, chattering to herself. I smiled at her and mentally added to my list:

✶ *First time meeting a real, live spider monkey*
✶ *First Maya ruins*

Ancient Ruins

⊚

I was so thrilled to have Fuzz at my side that I was taken by surprise when the road ended at a grassy clearing and the ruins loomed into view.

"Oh—wow!"

Giant limestone steps led to a series of pyramid-shaped ruins that stood brilliant white in the hot sun. One pyramid, larger than all the rest, seemed to touch the blue sky. The open area in front of the pyramids formed a vast, grassy courtyard. Together, the courtyard and surrounding ruins stretched into the distance. I couldn't wait to explore!

Fuzz scurried along the grass between two soccer nets set up in the clearing we were crossing. *Soccer nets?* That was a good sign! Fuzz ran in the direction of about a dozen small thatched-roofed huts with no walls.

"Fuzz, wait!" I called, jogging after her. "Wait up!"

She raced past a solar grid, a satellite dish, a basketball hoop, and a cluster of palm trees. Along the way, several college-age students in bandannas, shorts, and tank tops pushed wheelbarrows full of dirt. They said hi, but I didn't see anyone my age.

A young man drove a beat-up moped across the

grass. Fuzz scampered toward him, and when he slowed to a stop, she hopped into his basket. They both waved as they drove off.

"Huh," I said, feeling a little zing of rejection. I wouldn't have minded a ride, myself.

I spotted the Jeep at the edge of the camp. Mom, Dad, and Mr. Bol were unloading our gear beside yet another thatched-roofed hut, this one with sides.

"Hey, Jess," Dad asked as I approached. "What do you think of our new home?" He opened the screen door for me.

"Well, it's nothing like Whitman Street!" I said, picturing our two-story brick house with green shutters. I looked around and noted the dirt floor, two simple wooden tables and chairs and a blue tarp in the corner, hung from pieces of twine.

"What's that?" I wondered aloud.

"Our shower stall," Mom said. She pointed to a large black plastic bag that hung outside the window. "The sun warms the water in the bag, and we use that water for our showers. It's called a sun shower."

Across from a simple double bed stood bunk beds built of peeled tree trunks. "I get the top!" I said, joking. If Jason and Heather had been here they would have had first pick. With a little pang, I missed them all over again.

Just then, Fuzz raced through the open door and climbed the bunk's log frame to the top bunk. "You're back!" I said, glad that she'd returned.

Mom laughed. "Looks like your little friend beat you to the top." And sure enough, Fuzz was peering down from *my* bed.

"Hey, who do you think you are? I get first dibs. I'm older."

3

Alone

Within two weeks, I had developed a routine. First thing every morning, I shook out my shoes, just in case one of them had become a new home for a scorpion. Then I headed for breakfast at the "Café Cabana," a fancy name for the simple cook hut.

The camp cooks were from Benque Viejo, near the border with Guatemala. They served up wonderful meals—fried tortillas with sugar called *fryjacks*, eggs, fresh-squeezed orange juice, tamales in banana leaves, and watermelon. They spoke very little English, so I had a chance to use the little bit of Spanish I'd learned at school. I thanked them at every meal with a *"Muchas gracias!"* and hoped that by the time we returned to Michigan, I would be able to speak a little more Spanish.

After breakfast, I went back to our hut and sat down at my table with my schoolbooks while the dig teams left for their various work sites. Mom had explained to my teacher back home that going to Belize was a once-in-a-lifetime opportunity for me, and Miss Mattila had agreed. She had arranged a half-year's worth of fourth-grade

schoolwork into assignments that I could do pretty much
on my own. Mom helped me with math and science and
Dad helped with social studies and geography, but I
found that I could in fact do most of the work by myself.
Dad was also teaching me to play the guitar, so his guitar
lessons were my music class. We had electricity only when
the camp generator was on, so that was when I used my
parents' laptop to send written assignments by e-mail to
Miss Mattila for correction and grading. I usually sent
e-mails to my friends and to Heather, Jason, and Grandma
Emi at the same time, so I was doing a lot of writing. All
in all, our specialized form of home-schooling proved to
be pretty workable.

After lunch, or whenever I finished my schoolwork, I climbed up and down the pyramid steps until
my thighs burned. That was my gym class. At the top of
the ruins, huge stucco tablets formed a *frieze,* which was
a sculptured band at the top of the wall. I studied the
ancient tablets and tried to imagine the long-ago rulers
with feathery headgear and wild beasts at their feet. I
wondered about the people who had actually built the
pyramids and those who had sculpted the tablets—the
same tablets Mom and Dad were restoring.

Often I rested in the shade of an upper tower
and gazed across the jungle and farmlands—and could

see almost to the ocean. Sometimes I imagined myself a Maya princess. As a member of the nobility, I was one of the few allowed at the top of the ruins.

The rest of the time I roamed around camp. When the researchers weren't huddled in holes measured out in the ground, called *quadrants,* they worked side by side at big tables and washtubs in the shade of the huts. They spent hours brushing off the artifacts they found—washing, drying, tagging, photographing, and bagging bits of pottery and bones. I helped, too.

Late afternoons, after the heat of the day let up but before dinner, the crew often gathered for a game of soccer, and they always included me. Many of my goals were easy goals—ones they let through to give me a break—but I was happy just to be playing. Then, every evening, the whole crew ate outside together at long tables under the stars, laughing and talking by candlelight about the day's work or about past digs.

"I was on a dig in northern New Mexico," one college girl explained, her long blonde hair held in a twist by a pencil. "Just like here, I thought for days that the dig was going nowhere. Then I had this major fight with my boyfriend and went off to sit on a ledge—you know, to cool off. There I was, fuming, and lo and behold, I saw this little piece of bone sticking out from the ridge

Sometimes I imagined myself a Maya princess.

below me! It turned the whole dig around! And as for
that boyfriend, well, he's history now, too," she said
with a laugh.

"Something exactly like that happened to me!" a
man at the other end of the table exclaimed. "But it was
at a site in Kenya . . . "

The crew laughed and talked on into the night,
moving from the tables to the bonfire. I always listened
for what my parents would say, but they didn't seem
to tell as many stories as some of the others did. Still,
they clearly enjoyed being part of the team and often
stayed by the bonfire long after I went to bed. Most
nights, I fell asleep to the sounds of boisterous laughter
mingling with the sounds of the jungle.

Fuzz had come to visit me while I worked at my
table in our hut. She climbed on the bed and examined
Toshi while I looked through the photo album that my
class had given me at my surprise going-away party. I
didn't want to complain, but I was beginning to miss my
friends back home. What were they doing in class at this
very moment? Having a spider monkey to talk to was
great, but I missed having someone my own age—

and my own species!—to hang out with.

Suddenly, something landed on my head. Fuzz had moved to my table and was emptying my pen and pencil holder by throwing everything across the room—and making a terrible racket. When she pulled a pen apart and left a trail of blue ink across my math paper, I stood up. She jumped from the corner of the table back to the bed and then climbed back up to the top bunk.

"That's it!" I said. "You're right, Fuzz. It's time to play."

I blotted up the ink mess with a rag, then opened the door. "Let's go see what Mom and Dad are up to." Fuzz scooted ahead of me into the bright midday sun.

We stepped back into the shade when we reached my parents' research hut, where dozens of stucco tablets like the ones at the tops of the ruins lay on wooden pallets. Elaborately sculpted, some showed early Maya with flattened foreheads. If I'd grown up then, I would have had to wear a board strapped to my forehead until I was six years old! Back then, people admired slanted foreheads—sleek as a jaguar's. I'd also learned that children of nobility were trained to be cross-eyed for the same reason—it was considered attractive. Parents would hang a single bright jewel in front of a baby's eyes until the child saw double. I made my eyes cross, just to try out the feeling.

"Mom?" I said, seeing her in double.

Mom lifted her gaze from a tablet, her black braid hanging over her shoulder. "Hi, honey," she said. Then she laughed. "Oh, Jess, you're so goofy!"

I let my eyes return to normal. *There. Much better.*

"Done with your schoolwork already?" she asked. I could see from the grid paper in her hand that she was trying to fill in the missing lines of the design—and Maya history.

"Yup."

"Isn't that great? Now you have the rest of the day free to do whatever you want."

"Fuzz wants to play."

"That's good. I'm glad you have a friend."

"She's cute and I like her and all that, but—"

"Yes?"

"Just wondering. Want to kick the soccer ball around with me for a while?"

She glanced at the stucco tablet, then at her grid paper. "Sure. But in just a few minutes. I'm so close to figuring out some of the missing pieces right now. It's like a puzzle, and you know how it is when you're close? When your brain is working so hard that you don't want to stop right in the middle?"

Alone

Inside, my tiny bit of loneliness turned to a big knot in my throat.

"Sure." My shoulders sagged. "That's okay."

I scooted around to Dad and the whiter, newer tablets. Whenever original stucco tablets fell to the ground these days, they were replaced by lighter, more durable replicas made of fiberglass. Then the crumbling originals were buried in the ground inside the pyramids to keep them from decaying further. Each replica tablet looked like a perfect match, only it was brighter.

Dad was leaning over one of the replica tablets, cupping his chin in his hand and tapping his nose with his forefinger. After the first few days of Belize sun, my fair-haired father had matched the "tourist trees," the ones with peeling reddish bark. Now, to protect his skin, he wore long khaki pants, a long-sleeved white shirt, and a wide-brimmed hat wherever he worked—in the sun and in the shade. All this, and sunscreen, too!

"Dad?" I asked, forcing a cheery smile. "Want to kick the ball around with me? You know, take a break?"

He motioned me closer and wrapped his free arm around my shoulders. "I'd love to, Jess, but I can't right now. I just opened this can of sealer so I can coat this fiberglass replica—"

I bristled and jerked away from him. "But Dad,

these things are all *old* things—dead things. I'm here now. I'm *alive!* I'm important, too."

"C'mon, Jess." He crossed his arms over his chest and met my eyes. "You knew going into this trip that a dig site means work. And the work *is* important. It's about our lives today as much as it's about the lives of people yesterday. The past informs the present. How people lived back then—what they *did*—helps us understand people now. Ourselves, and others."

I let out a quiet sigh. I wanted to be treated as his daughter, not one of his research students.

"Of course, you're important to me, Jess—you know that—but I have to get my work done before I can join you to play."

"Yeah, I know. It's okay," I said, turning away and pretending to be interested in the tablets so that he couldn't see my face. "I'm sorry." That's what I said, but inside, my heart sank. It's not as though my parents hadn't been spending lots of time showing me the ruins, exploring every burial tomb and damp passageway, and climbing up and down the pyramids with me. By now I knew enough so that I could probably give tours, just like the guides did for the tourists who visited Caracol every day. And although I saw kids on tours and waved to some, no one ever stayed. When the park closed, everything went back to feeling as if the ruins belonged to us, the dig site team—with me the only kid.

"Hey, Jess, we can kick the ball around before supper, okay?"

"Yeah, okay," I said, biting back my disappointment as I stepped outside.

I didn't want to appear long-faced. I mean, this *was* the adventure of my lifetime. Every day the ruins gleamed magically in the sun. Every night I fell asleep on my top bunk listening to the chorus of jungle sounds—frogs and toads and all the things that go bump in the night. Toucans and parrots woke me with their chatter. I even got to watch a pair of bright green parrots feed their young every day in the hole-riddled tree right outside our hut.

To complain would have been babyish. And I was not going to act like a baby, no matter what.

"Fuzz," I said, glancing at her. "How about you and me? Ready for a little soccer practice?"

From a nearby storage shed, I grabbed a soccer ball, and Fuzz and I headed to the makeshift soccer field. At the ruins beyond, tourists clustered around guides.

Fuzz climbed to the top of one of the goalie nets. "Stay there," I said. "You can watch me slam 'em in."

Fuzz watched me for only a few seconds, then

jumped off and raced toward Café Cabana, no doubt in search of handouts.

My shoulders sagged. *Alone again.* At home, I had a soccer team, I had friends, and I even had my sister and brother. Here there was no one. Even Fuzz had deserted me again.

"Okay then," I said under my breath, trying to shrug off the loneliness. "Time for that amazing goal."

I set the ball down twenty yards from the net, then backed up several feet and ran at it. As I neared the ball, I let loose with my right foot. Problem was, my mind wasn't on the game—a game of one. The moment my foot met the ball, I flew up into the air, and then I landed on my elbow and tailbone.

"Oomph!" My backside stung. I lay there for a minute, hoping that I hadn't broken or injured anything important—other than my pride. When I looked up, I saw to my amazement that the ball was *right* where I wanted it to be—smack-dab in the center of the net. A miracle! But more amazing still, just a few feet from the net stood a girl. A girl about my age.

"Hi," she called. Brown bangs skimmed her dark eyes. Above her bright yellow shorts, she wore a dark orange T-shirt.

"My name's Sarita. Need a goalie?"

4

A Friend

"Go ahead," called Sarita. "Kick it again."

"I'll try to stay on my feet this time," I joked. Then, aiming for the net, I kicked hard. The ball zoomed toward the right inside corner, but Sarita bent her knees and skillfully stopped it.

"Perfect block!" I called. "That was a great stop!"

"And a good kick!" she called back.

While the sun beat down, we took turns trying to score on each other. When I felt as hot as a twice-baked potato, I pointed toward the huts. "I'm dying! Let's get some water."

As we approached our hut, Fuzz scooted along the ground toward us. She sat on her haunches and peered up at Sarita.

"Look, Fuzz likes you," I said.

"She'd better!" Sarita said. "We've known each other a long time. How ya doing, Fuzz?"

Fuzz chattered at Sarita as if she were telling her all about her day, then turned and ran off across the field.

I raised my eyebrows in question.

"My papa's a guide." Sarita tilted her head toward the ruins. "Sometimes he brings me along."

"Michael Bol?" I handed her a bottle of water.

Her chocolate eyes widened. "How'd you know?"

"'Expect the unexpected,'" I said with a smile.

"That's what Papa always says!" Sarita grinned.

After drinking our fill, we kicked the ball back and forth under the shade of towering palm trees. Sarita told me that English was her first language, but she also spoke Spanish and Mayan, which she mainly used at home with her family. She was ten, same age as me. She was in Standard Four, which was the same as fourth grade, and she was on winter break from the School of the Sacred Heart. She had three younger brothers, and seven chickens, and she used to have a dog. I told her about Jason and Heather and Grandma Emi, and about my school.

We strolled to the ancient Maya ball court and took turns kicking the soccer ball up the two grassy slopes. "It's weird to think that ancient Mayas once played here, one-on-one, like we're doing," I said. The heat was getting to me again. I stopped and squatted beside the round stone in the center of the court, tracing its worn engravings with my forefinger.

Sarita joined me. "I guess a player used his elbows,

his legs, and his whole body—except his hands," she
said. "It must have been a hard game. Their ball was
heavier and they used hoops."

I scrunched up my face. "Yeah—and the loser
lost his life."

"And—" Sarita added, her eyes widening, "all the
people in the loser's kingdom became *slaves* to the winner.
Good thing some things have changed!"

"That's for sure," I said. "My soccer team back
home would be in big trouble this year."

Suddenly, shrill yet deep-throated sounds thun-
dered through the treetops. It sounded as though
300-pound gorillas, bellowing and shrieking, were ready
to attack! I grabbed Sarita's arm. "Sarita! What is that?
Let's get out of here!"

But Sarita didn't run. She didn't even look scared.
Instead, she tilted her head and said, "Don't worry. It's
just howler monkeys."

"I've heard howler monkeys before, but they
weren't like this! Are you sure?"

"When they're a long ways away they usually
sound different. Softer. These are closer."

"And ready to attack us!" I jumped up.

She shook her head. "They just *sound* big! They're
not much bigger than Fuzz."

I glanced into the treetops. I didn't see a single monkey, yet the bellowing sound continued, growing louder and sending shivers to my toes. Most jungle sounds were pleasant, but this one was *eerie*.

Sarita stood up beside me. "The howlers won't hurt us, but a storm might."

"I don't get it."

"When the howler monkeys send up a racket, a storm usually follows," Sarita declared with certainty. "Just watch."

And just like that, a breeze tickled the palm trees and kicked up a brisk wind.

"See?" Sarita said, taking off at a run. I raced alongside her and together we darted into our hut. We climbed to my top bunk and sat side by side, dangling our legs over the edge of the bed and talking as the wind and rain picked up.

Fat raindrops splattered the sand path outside the hut. Then the rain began to fall hard, blown sideways by a monster wind. It fell so fast and so hard that one moment I could see across to the hut where my parents were working, and the next, I could see only as far as the hole-riddled tree several yards away.

We were in the tropics and I'd come to expect brief rains most every afternoon, but this was the hardest rain

yet. When it got so that Sarita and I could no longer hear each other's words, I jumped down from the bunk to lower the window coverings on the side where the rain was starting to come in.

Creak, crack, slam!

Sarita scrambled off the bunk and we crouched on the dirt floor, ready to take cover under the tables. I looked around. The roof was still on. But something outside the hut was wrong. I stood up and peeked out the door. "The tree—look! It's down. That's the one where the parrots are nesting. What if their babies are hurt?"

I dashed into the pouring rain. "Sarita, we have to find them!"

From behind, she called back, "Jess, wait!"

There was no time to wait. I splashed through puddles to the toppled tree. It had snapped in several places and its limbs were now scattered across the grass. Rain and wind pounded my body. I spotted something flopping about in a pool of water. It was a baby parrot. If it had siblings, I couldn't see them.

I scooped the baby parrot close to my chest. "You need help." I nearly slipped headfirst in the mud, but I made it back to the door. I was drenched to the skin.

"Oh—" Sarita said, holding the door for me. "Now I see."

"I've been watching the parents bring food to a hole in that tree since we came here. I knew there had to be babies, but I found only this one." Rain dripped from my nose, my ears, and my braids.

Sarita peered more closely at the raggedy bird cupped in my hands. It shook its thin coat of soggy feathers and wobbled unsteadily. Its beak and head seemed too large for its scrawny little body.

"I was too scared to go after you," Sarita said. "You know, Jess, other creatures nest in a tree like that, too."

"Like what?"

"Like tarantulas, for starters."

A Friend

A tingle shot up my neck and I shuddered. "I never even thought about it—tarantulas?"

"They like hollows for nesting, too." She touched my shoulder. "It's okay, Jess. You're safe. And because of you, this little parrot is, too."

"Yeah, but I don't want to be stupid, either."

"You're not stupid. You just didn't know, that's all."

I flashed Sarita a grateful smile, then studied the little bird in my hands. It looked up at me and opened its beak wide.

Sarita giggled. "Looks like it's hungry."

"I don't know anything about feeding a baby parrot. Do you?"

"When the rain stops, we can ask Barbara. She's an expert on everything," Sarita said with certainty.

I found the shoulder bag I'd bought as a gift for Heather and lined it with a washcloth. I'd find something else for her later. "It's not exactly a nest," I explained as I lowered the parrot inside, "but it will have to do." The little bird squawked softly, and then huddled into its new nest and closed its eyes.

Behind the blue tarp, I changed into dry clothes. Then I joined Sarita on the top bunk again. We swung our legs with the baby parrot between us.

When the rain let up and the winds died down,

we tromped over wet grass and along the muddy road to the ranger station. Barbara turned from her computer screen. "Hello, girls. What can I do for you?"

Sarita explained about the fallen tree and the baby parrot, and I lifted the flap to the shoulder bag. The baby parrot lifted its head and peered out.

"Things have been crazy-busy around here," Barbara said, studying the parrot. "How would you girls like to take care of this bird until the experts at the Belize Zoo can get here and take it?"

I met Sarita's eyes and we both nodded.

"I'm not saying it can be your pet, you under-stand—it's a wild bird."

"We understand," I said. "We just want to help."

"Okay, follow me." She led the way to a storage room filled with supplies and shelves of books. "Every year or two, it seems, we end up with an orphaned par-rot on our hands." She examined the books, picked one out, and then began to flip through its pages. "Here we go. Looks like this mealy parrot is in the late transitional phase. See how its feathering is quite advanced? It will soon be walking well, and climbing, too. It's going to need plenty of rest, just like a human baby, and most likely you'll do two feedings per day."

"Two feedings per day," I repeated, taking our job

seriously. "But when, exactly?"

"Early morning and before sundown. Think you girls are up to that responsibility?"

"Yes!" we said in unison.

"This little parrot is old enough to adapt to being fed by humans, but don't expect him or her to be tame," Barbara said. She sent us off with a book, a box of sugarless dry cereal, fruits and vegetables to dice into small pieces, and a lidded bucket of small pellets for parrots.

When we met up with Mr. Bol and my parents, our arms were full. They glanced questioningly at all our supplies and the bulging, wiggling shoulder bag. Carefully, with my hand over the parrot's wings, I drew it out gently—just the way Barbara had shown us—and put it on my shoulder. It wobbled slightly and nibbled at my braid.

Mom tilted her head. "I think it's a bird, but don't keep us in suspense."

First I introduced Sarita to Mom and Dad. Then together we explained how we came to be in charge of a baby parrot.

Sarita turned to her dad. "Barbara said we're 'officially in charge' of it for now."

"But Jess lives here at the camp, and you live at Iguana Creek," Mr. Bol said. "I don't quite see how you can *both* be in charge of the same bird."

"Um, we were thinking that we could take turns keeping the parrot," I said. Actually, we hadn't discussed this yet, but I thought it might be a good plan.

Sarita beamed. "Exactly our plan," she said.

"Your mama needs your help already," Mr. Bol said. "Little Luciano is a handful. A wild creature like this is a big responsibility. Are you sure?"

"Papa," she said matter-of-factly. "I'm ten. I can handle it."

Sarita understood completely about being ten and we hadn't even talked about it. I wanted to jump and touch my toes with one of those cheerleader flying-splits moves. While I waited for the powers-that-be to make a decision, I silently added to my list:

* *First time rescuing a baby parrot*
* *First friend in Belize*

Mr. Bol squared his arms. "Okay. You girls work out taking turns with the parrot—at least until school starts up again for Sarita in a week."

Dad agreed. "And Jess, it can be part of your schoolwork, too."

Mom winked at me.

A Friend

"Time to go." Mr. Bol put his hands on Sarita's shoulders, then turned back. "By the way," he said. "I have clients coming in from Texas, and they want to spend most of tomorrow here at Caracol. If her mother can spare her, perhaps I could bring Sarita back to help out with that baby parrot. Would that be okay with you, Miss Jess?"

Sarita smiled.

I couldn't have been happier. "Absolutely, Mr. Bol!"

5

Fire Ants

The next day, just as I was finishing up my multiplication problems, Sarita knocked on the door. Happy down to my flip-flops to see my new friend again, I called, "Come on in!"

It's funny. On past digs, I'd never been lonely. While Mom and Dad worked, I was with Heather and Jason. We played cards, Scrabble, and MadLibs, and we went on adventure hikes. Now I realized how lucky I'd been to have them, even with all their teasing. Without them, a big hole—like the cenotes that held water for ancient Mayas—had seemed to grow bigger inside me every day. Until yesterday.

With a swipe of the back of her hand, Sarita flipped up her bangs, accenting her wide eyes. "It's a lot cooler in here than out in the sun."

"For me," I said, snapping my book shut with a clap and putting my assignment away in a folder, "it's hot *everywhere.*"

Sarita glanced around. "So, how's our baby doing?"

I pointed to the top bunk. The shoulder bag was

open and heaped around the parrot like a nest. Sarita stepped closer, stood on her tiptoes, and peered in. I joined her and put my finger to my lips. *"Shh.* She woke us up at dawn squawking," I whispered. "What do you think we should call her?"

"Her?" Sarita asked.

"Well, why not? Barbara didn't seem to know and I hate saying 'it,' so let's just say it's a 'she.'"

"Hmm," Sarita said. "Okay, but she does need a name. How about Crackers?"

"Or Polly," I suggested.

"How about Pepper?"

"Hmm, pepper makes my nose itch." I tucked a loose strand of hair back into one of my pigtail braids and sighed.

Sarita beamed. "I know! I read a book once about a girl named Pippi Longstocking. I loved it! What do you think of Pippi?"

I studied our little parrot. "Pippi," I repeated, trying it out. "Yeah, I like that." Then I came up with a tongue twister, the kind I used to make up with Heather and Jason. I said with a grin, "Pippi is positively perfect for our pretty little parrot."

Sarita laughed.

"Try saying that three times," I said, and she did.

We took turns bumbling over the words and made up some new tongue twisters, too. Then we left Pippi asleep in her bag and stepped outside.

Across the field and outside my parents' research hut, Mr. Bol stood with Mom and Dad. They waved to us. "Sarita, is your dad leaving already? You just got here," I said, unable to hide the disappointment in my voice. "I don't want you to go."

"Me either. I thought Mr. and Mrs. Cutwell—those are the tourists with him—said they wanted to spend the whole day here."

Reluctantly, we walked across the sunlit field toward our parents.

Dad took off his safari hat, sporting red from his nose down and white from his nose up. "Girls, we have a plan to discuss with you."

"First," Mom said, graciously extending her palm toward me and addressing the older couple, "this is my daughter, Jess. And Jess, these are Mr. and Mrs. Cutwell from Austin, Texas."

"Nice to meet you," I said.

"They said they'd be happy to let you girls join them on their eco-adventure tour with Mr. Bol," Mom said, her eyes shining.

Mrs. Cutwell nodded at me, her white ponytail

pulled back, reminding me of Jane Goodall, the woman who studied monkeys—or was it gorillas?—in Africa.

"That's right," Mr. Cutwell added, running his hand over the top of his perfectly groomed gray hair.

"Eco-adventure?" I repeated. Anything with the word "adventure" sounded great to me, as long as I didn't think too much about snakes, scorpions, and tarantulas. "Both of us? When? For how long?"

"Well, for most of the next five days," Mr. Bol explained. "Some of the time we'll all be camping out—and some of the time you girls will stay at our home with Sarita's mother."

Dad smiled at me. "You'll have a chance to see Sarita's home and meet her family," he said, "plus you'll get to explore some caves. This can be another part of your science curriculum." He turned to the Cutwells, who had moved toward the original stucco tablets in the research area. "Bob and Marianne," he said, "are you *sure* this isn't an imposition?"

Mrs. Cutwell waved away his concern. "Bob and I weren't blessed with children or grandchildren, so it would be mighty fine to have the girls along."

I was getting excited, but then I remembered. "Oh, but we can't."

"Why not?" Sarita's smile fell.

"Pippi. She needs to be fed morning and night."

"Oh, that's right."

Mr. Bol brought his hands together in a solid clap. "Hey, we're part of the jungle and the jungle is part of us. Bring that bird along. Most of the time you can keep on caring for your little parrot, and when you can't, I bet Sarita's brothers will take care of it."

Sarita's face scrunched with worry. "Papa, I don't think they're old enough to—"

"Don't worry," he said. "It'll work out."

Mom looked to Dad. I could tell that they were having one of their silent talks. She raised her eyebrows. He shook his head and then turned to me. "We wish that we could take care of the bird, but I'm afraid this isn't the best time for us." Dad glanced around at the tablets, as if that explained everything. "If Mr. Bol thinks it will work to take the parrot along to their house, then you'd better go pack."

I turned, and headed toward our hut. But after just a few steps into the field, I shrieked.

"Ouch! Ouch! Ouch!" I danced and twirled and spun back toward my parents, slapping my feet and ankles the whole way. When I looked down, three fire ants clung fiercely to my skin. I batted them off.

"Oh, honey," Dad said, putting his arm around

my shoulder. "I thought you knew about the fire ants' highway across this field. Are you okay?"

Tears pooled in my eyes. The red spots burned and hurt as much as hornet stings. But I was determined not to start crying like a baby. If I did, maybe everyone would re-think the whole idea of taking me along on the eco-adventure.

"I'm . . . I'm okay," I stuttered.

From inside the research hut, Mom produced a first-aid kit and a wooden folding chair. She motioned for me to sit. I sniffed and clenched my teeth as she knelt in front of me and wiped some kind of ointment on the red spots. "This will help."

"Thanks," I managed, glad for some babying. "I knew they crossed this field, but Dad's right—I forgot about them."

Mom patted my knee and said, "You probably won't forget again."

"That's for sure," I said, feeling really stupid for forgetting.

Then she said quietly, "And Jess, Sarita's home will be different from homes in Houghton."

"Mom, I know."

"And even though Sarita's dad is one of the best guides around, you will need to be extra careful. Pay close attention and—"

"Mom, I'm not a—" I started, then stopped and washed the whine out of my voice. "I'm ten, Mom. I'll be careful." I stood up. "Want to come help me pack?"

As we headed to the hut, I reluctantly added to my list:

✗ *First time getting bitten by fire ants*

6

Sarita's Home

I couldn't wait to go. I packed some clothes, sunscreen, my toothbrush and toothpaste, and my camera. Dad reminded me to take lots of photos to e-mail to my class and to Heather, Jason, and Grandma Emi. Just before we left, I snapped a photo of Mom and Dad, with Fuzz sitting between them, in the clearing.

With Pippi in her bag, Sarita and I squeezed together in the backseat with Mrs. Cutwell, who spent more time with her head in a book than looking out the window. Luckily, Pippi napped in her nest during the hottest hours of the day.

Along a river road, I spotted a four-foot-long crocodile sunning itself on a muddy bank. Above the water, iguanas stretched themselves along tree branches.

"See that one?" I pointed the camera and clicked.

"There's another one over there," Sarita said.

Their greenish-brown, scaly bodies blended in perfectly with branches and leaves. Some were small, only a few inches long, but others were several feet long from nose to tail. One dove from its branch right into the water below, then swished along the surface. I added it to my list: *First time seeing iguanas and crocodiles in the wild.*

We drove on, windows down. The warm air blew across my face, just as hot as when I'd arrived but now easier for me to handle. Between vast stretches of dark, dense jungle, sunlight cut into open fields. Some fields were green with crops, while others were charred and smoldering. The air in Belize, I realized, often carried a hint of smoke.

We followed a winding road to the Paradise Jungle Lodge, where we dropped off the Cutwells. Mr. Cutwell tipped his hat. "We're fixin' to see you bright and early tomorrow morning, Michael."

"I'll be back before you've had your first cup of coffee," Mr. Bol said with a deep laugh. Then Sarita climbed into the front seat next to her father, and we drove off.

Soon, Mr. Bol turned into a small clearing at the base of a hill and parked the Jeep. Stone steps and a wooden handrail led from the road halfway up the hill to a couple of small huts with tin roofs. Sheets fluttered on a clothesline strung between trees.

"We're home," Mr. Bol said. "Grab your things, girls. Tomorrow you'll stay here while I'm with the Cutwells, so don't leave anything behind in the Jeep."

For a second, my stomach fluttered. Mom had been right when she said it would not be like a house in Houghton. Well, this would be another "first" for me: *My first visit to a Maya home.*

"Okay, let me get a picture," I said. Sarita posed for me, one hand on the wooden railing, her head tilted, her home rising in the background.

Exactly thirty-two stone steps later, we stood under the flat metal awning of a simple hut. A colorful hammock and a woven chair hung between the awning's posts. From the open doorway, two barefoot boys peered out. The moment they spotted Mr. Bol, they ran and flung themselves around his legs. Then, seeing me, they shyly stepped back toward the hut.

"No, stay here, boys," Mr. Bol said. Then he proudly introduced them. "This is Marcos. He's seven. And this is José. He's five. Boys, this is Jess."

A woman in a colorful dress and blue flip-flops stepped out. She carried a baby in the crook of her arm. "And this is Yollie, my lovely wife," Mr. Bol said.

"I'm so pleased to meet you," she said, her words warm and welcoming. She wrapped one arm around Sarita's shoulder. "Sarita told me all about you when she came home yesterday. She couldn't stop talking."

That brought a smile to my lips. Maybe Sarita

had been hoping for a friend, too!

Mrs. Bol handed the baby to Sarita. "Will you hold Luke and rock him if he fusses, while I finish dinner?"

"Yes, Mama." Sarita handed the shoulder bag to me with *our* sleeping baby inside. She put her fingers to her lips. I took that to mean that we'd explain about Pippi later, and I gently adjusted the bag over my shoulder.

Wearing only little red shorts, Sarita's baby brother smiled up at her, fingering her bangs with both hands. "And this is Luciano—but we call him Luke, our little bundle of trouble." Sarita rubbed her nose lightly across his. "Don't we?" she cooed.

"How old is he?" I asked, tickling his tiny toes and watching his little, round face blossom into smiles.

"Nine months." Sarita laid him in the hammock sideways and, standing beside it, rocked him back and forth until his eyes could not stay open any longer. He looked snug and happy.

"Dinner's ready!"

We left little Luke sleeping under the awning and stepped through the doorway into a dark hut with a dirt floor. It held a wooden table, kitchen supplies, a metal cupboard, and a large clay stove on stilts in one corner. Not a single bed. Where were we supposed to sleep?

Mrs. Bol stood beside the wood-fired stove, patting tortillas into shape and laying them on the hot surface. Delicious smells rose with the smoke, which seeped through the cracks in the wood walls and out the bare windows. She stirred something in a pot that made my stomach grumble. I was hungrier than I'd realized.

"Let's eat before Luke wakes up," Mrs. Bol said. The table was already set. "Please sit," she said and ladled chicken-and-onion soup into our bowls. She set a plate of warm corn tortillas in the center of the table. Nothing had ever tasted better.

After dinner, Sarita and I showed off Pippi to the Bol family. The boys were interested for a few minutes, but then they dashed away with dull machete knives in hand. I couldn't believe it—machetes!

Sarita must have read my face. "Here, living in the jungle," she explained, "we get small, dull machetes when we're little—so we can learn to handle them."

"But why?"

"To chop paths, to make kindling, all kinds of things. It's a tool."

"Do you have one?"

She looked over her shoulder at me and smiled,

and I didn't know if she meant "of course" or "that's silly." I felt too stupid to ask.

We fed Pippi and then clipped her shoulder bag to the clothesline. She peeked out, squawked, and then disappeared into her nest again while we washed the dishes by hand. As we worked, the boys raced in and out. Mr. Bol relaxed in the hanging chair, his pipe cupped in his hands, and Mrs. Bol nursed the baby, her blouse open. I was embarrassed and tried not to look, but then I realized that no one but me seemed uncomfortable. In Belize, I reminded myself, many things were different from what I was used to in Houghton.

After we finished the dishes, Sarita opened a metal cupboard filled with textbooks and papers. "This is where I keep my schoolwork," she said proudly. "Mama wants me to be a teacher, just like her."

I glanced out toward where Sarita's mom was sitting with the baby.

"Oh, she used to teach high school kids until her own kids came along. She plans to go back someday. Her sister thinks she should live in the city and be more modern. But we like living the old way, the Maya way. But when I grow up," she continued, "I want to study in the United States and be a doctor who works with kids— a pediatrician. What do you want to be?"

"I don't know what I want to do," I said. "Maybe become a professional soccer player, or a snowboarder." I laughed. "I don't really know yet!"

I wondered where we were going to sleep, but Sarita answered that question before I could ask it.

"Let's go up to the house," she said and led me a short distance up the hill to a newer wooden building on cement blocks. It too was simple, but it had a door and screened windows and a wooden floor. Inside, two sets of narrow bunks, much like the ones at the camp, lined one wall. A hammock swung across the corner.

"You can take the hammock tonight," Sarita said. I looked at the hammock. I was supposed to sleep in it—all night?

She pointed to a partitioned room. "And my mama and papa sleep in there."

Standing on a real wood floor for the first time in weeks, I felt as though I'd arrived at a grand hotel!

⑨

A rooster's crowing, shrill and insistent, woke me. I turned in the hammock, setting it swinging slightly. I couldn't believe that I'd slept so well. Maybe I'd bring a hammock back to Houghton, to use instead of a bed.

And one for Heather, too.

Sarita stirred in her bunk and faced me. Her eyes opened. "Hi," she whispered.

"Hi," I said softly.

From the partitioned bedroom Sarita's mom called, "Before you and Jess run off, Sarita, don't forget the chickens—and remember, it's wash day, too."

"Yes, Mama."

"I can help," I whispered.

"No, you don't have to."

"Really, I don't mind. I help lots at home, too."

I'd never scattered feed for chickens before: *First time feeding chickens.*

Doing wash at Sarita's was a lot different from doing wash at home. After breakfast, we hauled empty metal buckets down the hill and across the dirt road to a water pump. We took turns at the pump handle, and when the buckets were full, we carried them up the 32 steps to the back of the cook hut. In a large metal washtub, we rubbed the clothes against a scrub board until they were clean. My fingers puckered and turned red from being in the water so long. Then we rinsed all the things in another tub of clear water, squeezed them out, and piled them in a plastic laundry basket.

Next we headed to the clothesline with the heavy basket of clean clothes. The sun was high in the sky and it burned my scalp. Sweat ran down my back, but I could see that we were almost done. With wooden clothespins, we clipped up the laundry. We had even washed the cloth from Pippi's "nest," which was getting soiled and stinky. I hung that up to dry, too.

I turned to look at Pippi, who was watching us from a perch on the hammock rope. That's when my foot caught on a root.

I tripped, flew forward, and knocked over the basket of wet, clean laundry. The basket did perfect cartwheels across the reddish ground until it stopped at a tree. Clothes lay scattered in its path.

"Oh no!" I started scooping them up, but realized that they were all muddy with red dirt. "I'm sorry!"

I wanted to jump in a cool, deep lake somewhere, to play—to do something *fun*. Not to do laundry anymore. I'd had enough! "Do we have to wash it all again?" I asked in exasperation, already knowing the answer.

If it had been Heather, she would have scolded me for not paying better attention. Mom would have sighed deeply. But Sarita just shrugged her shoulders. "You'd better *Belize* it," she said with a grin.

7

Caving

After finally finishing the laundry *again*, we had a lunch of beans, rice, and tortillas. Then we packed for our eco-adventure. Sarita's dad would return any minute. Sarita carried Pippi's shoulder bag into the cook hut.

A thin shaft of sunlight cut through the smoke-darkened hut and fell across the table where Mrs. Bol sat writing a letter. She looked up and said, "No, Sarita. You can't take that bird with you. It requires too much care, and it doesn't make any sense. What if you tip when you're on the water? You have to take better care of her."

Eyebrows raised, I glanced at Sarita. Did Mrs. Bol mean that we couldn't go, or that we couldn't bring Pippi?

Sarita kept her head half-bowed. "You mean . . . we can't go? But I've never been in a cave before."

"Well, neither have I," Mrs. Bol replied.

I studied Sarita and then her mother. How could anyone live so near caves and never explore them? Then I thought about scattering feed for the chickens, washing clothes by hand, splitting kindling, and the many chores that took so much time, and I understood better.

Caving

"Mama," Sarita tried again.

"Oh, well," Mrs. Bol said with a sigh. "There's always work to do, and you don't get opportunities like this very often. Marcos and José can help with the parrot. But I'll need a little extra help when you return."

"I promise!" Sarita crowed.

Sarita's mother took the bulging shoulder bag and hung it inside the hut. Pippi squawked. "Now go," Mrs. Bol said, kissing Sarita on the cheek. "And be careful."

Mr. Bol pulled up at the base of the hill and we climbed into the Jeep. Mrs. Cutwell's perfume was sweeter than garden flowers. She pointed up the hill. "You slept there?" she asked me quietly.

I guessed what she was thinking—that it looked rugged, even rough. I remembered thinking the same thing yesterday, yet I'd discovered that Sarita's simple home was warm and full of kindness. "Yes," I said proudly. "I love Sarita's home."

"Oh." And that was all she said before returning to her book. I noted its title, *Artifacts of Belize*. What was it with adults and artifacts? I'm sure it was interesting, but there was so much to see and learn about the here-and-now Belize, not just about artifacts and other things from the past.

As Mr. Bol explained to the Cutwells about the many

ethnic groups of Belize, from Mayas to Spaniards, from descendants of African slaves to Mennonites, I studied my reflection in the window. I was as much a mix of nationalities as many people were here in Belize. Both Belize and the States were melting pots, bringing together people from all over. I liked that. I glanced over at Sarita and smiled. And although she didn't know what I was thinking about, she smiled back. Like a friend.

The road dropped into a valley and between pastures, and we drove toward a sign that read "Barton Creek Cave."

"Ready for our first cave?" Mr. Bol asked everyone.

"Sure am!" Mr. Cutwell said from the front seat. "Only cave I've ever been in was the Carlsbad Caverns in New Mexico. Took an elevator down to start the tour."

"Well, I hate to disappoint you, but there are no elevators on this tour!" Mr. Bol glanced back at us. "That okay with you, Miss Jess?"

"Okay with me."

"Will there be artifacts?" asked Mrs. Cutwell, finally putting down her book.

"Of sorts," Mr. Bol replied.

We hiked a short distance to a pool of deep, clear water. Several canoes lined its edge. Beyond the pool a dark cave waited. It had a small opening that was just wide enough for a canoe to slip through.

"We're going in there?" Mrs. Cutwell crossed her arms over her tank top.

"If you would rather not," Mr. Bol said, "you can wait here until we return."

Vines wove from the top of a ridge down toward the cave entrance, curving and twining like a thousand snakes. I wouldn't want to stay behind, no matter how lush and green and beautiful the pool was.

Mrs. Cutwell's voice came out shaky. "Okay, I'll go, I'll go."

Mr. Bol paddled a large canoe with Mrs. Cutwell in the center and Mr. Cutwell at the bow. Sarita and I followed in another canoe. I took the stern since I'd canoed before, back in Houghton.

Inch by inch, we glided into the cave, leaving every trace of sunshine behind.

"It's creepy," I whispered as the inky darkness deepened ahead.

Before it was too dark to see, Mr. Bol motioned me to paddle alongside his canoe. He reached over and handed each of us a helmet with a spotlight. We turned the spotlights on, sending shadows fleeing.

"Oh, wow!" The cave was a mysterious world of its own. A cathedral. I whispered, "This is amazing!"

JESS

From beneath her helmet, Sarita flashed me a big smile. Mr. Bol flipped on the large spotlight that was in their canoe, further illuminating the cave, and we paddled in deeper.

Stalactites and shelves of stalagmites took on the shapes of pillars, curtains of silk, towering mushrooms, and icicles. Drip, drip, drip, drip, drip. The constant sound of dripping—the slow, never-ending sculpting of the cave—surrounded us.

"Look down," Mr. Bol said. "Shine your lights down in the water. See the catfish and crayfish?" Nearly transparent shapes flitted beneath our canoe.

"Creepy," I said. "They're colorless."

"And blind, too," he said, "from the lack of sun."

We paddled on, deeper. Our lights flickered across clusters of bats clinging to rocks above and beside us.

"As long as they don't start flying—" Mrs. Cutwell whined.

Just then, with a whoosh of air and a flutter of hundreds of wings, the bats flew over and around and past us. Mrs. Cutwell let out a piercing scream, then yelled, "Bob, you know I hate bats!"

I stayed still, hoping the bats would use their sonar skills. *Please, don't fly into me!* After a minute or so, the cave grew quiet and still once again, and we

Caving

paddled farther into the cave.

When the walls and ceiling narrowed, Sarita and I bent low to fit under the stalactites. The air grew thicker and particles of dust gathered densely in the light. Then when we could go no farther, we carefully turned our canoes around.

Halfway back, Mr. Bol motioned us to draw up beside him. "Turn off your lights, girls. For a few minutes," he whispered, "we're going to sit in the dark and listen to the music of the cave."

"Oh, I'm not sure I like that idea," muttered Mrs. Cutwell. "Is it necessary?"

"You wanted an eco-adventure, not an amusement-park vacation, right, dear?" asked Mr. Cutwell.

"Okay, okay. Get on with it!" She was getting crabbier by the moment.

Mr. Bol disconnected the battery cables of the larger canoe's spotlight.

In the complete darkness, my throat tightened and my heart thumped in my ears. For the first time, I had a sense of what it might be like to be blind. I opened and closed my eyes, trying to not let my fear of the dark turn into panic. I listened to my breath, to the cave's drip-drip-dripping and soft gurgles.

Then, someone started singing, and I was sure it

wasn't Mrs. Cutwell. It was Sarita, and her voice was as clear as a crystal bell, high and perfect. She sang with words I didn't understand. Her voice danced around us, echoing off the cave's ceiling and walls. Although darkness wrapped completely around me, I was amazed I didn't feel scared. *An angel is singing at my side.*

When Sarita stopped singing, I let out a deep breath. "That was so pretty," I whispered.

"I don't know why I did that." From her voice, I knew she was embarrassed. "Sometimes I sing when I'm afraid, but this place . . . it's different. I just had to—"

"Where did you learn to sing like that?"

"At church," she said, "in the choir."

I was almost disappointed when we turned our headlights back on and paddled out toward the growing light. I'd have to tell Heather and Jason that I'd calmly survived several minutes in the dark. But I wouldn't tell them about how Sarita sounded like an angel, because they'd tease me about that. That was one memory I wanted to keep to myself.

As we emerged from the cave, the daylight was blinding. Every color seemed more vivid. The vines and trees were greener and the sky reflected in the pool was bluer than before.

It was like seeing the world with brand-new eyes.

Caving

By nightfall, we arrived at the Rio Frio Cave. Dusk was settling, and we quickly set up camp and had a meal of grilled chicken and coconut rice. Then we hiked with flashlights along a small swift river leading to the cave. Suddenly the cave opening loomed ahead, a gaping black hole like the mouth of a giant. I was glad that Sarita and I would be tenting outside the cave and near the campfire. The cave looked way, way, *way* too creepy.

We climbed up over boulders and down over the giant's rocky "teeth." "This is where you'll be camping," Mr. Bol said to the Cutwells with a sweep of his arm toward the sandy peninsula inside the cave. "I got special permission for you to do so."

"No! I will *not* sleep in here!" Mrs. Cutwell shouted above the roar of water. Then she turned to her husband. "And don't tell me not to worry about bats! This is *not* my idea of a vacation!"

"Honey—" Mr. Cutwell said.

"Don't you 'honey' me right now," she said, spinning away from him and the cave's entrance.

So Mr. Bol changed the tenting plans. The Cutwells would tent near the campfire with him. He would strap a hammock between trees for himself. "And you girls," he said, "get to sleep in the cave."

"By ourselves?" Sarita asked. I heard the whine in her voice and wanted to whine right along with her. I had the feeling that if we put our hearts into it, we could make quite a chorus together.

"The sand makes a softer floor," he said, helping us set up the tent. It soon stood on its own like a nylon igloo. He set a small candle in the sand near the tent door and lit it. "Now, don't worry," he said. "You're perfectly safe here, despite all Mrs. Cutwell's worries. This is an adventure, remember? And I'm not far away." He kissed the top of Sarita's head. "Get some sleep. Tomorrow will be another busy day."

We watched him climb out over the boulders and disappear.

I turned to Sarita. "We're in the belly of a giant!"

"I'm really scared!" she said.

I thought she might start crying, so I acted brave to help her—and me. "Me too," I said. "But we can do this." Beneath the cave's high dome, the candle cast our shadows up against the walls. They towered at least one hundred feet above us.

"Look, Sarita! We're giants!"

"Oh! We're huge!"

Caving

"Look, Sarita! We're giants!"

I stretched out my arms, and my shadow held up the cave's massive ceiling. Sarita hung her arms down and imitated a monkey. Then we both made stretching shadows, dancing shadows, twirling shadows, laughing shadows. Finally, we stopped to catch our breath and turned to our tent.

"Should we leave the candle lit?" I asked Sarita. "Just in case."

"Good idea."

Then we climbed into the tent, zipped our door securely shut, and changed into our pajamas. We made pillows out of our clothes and tucked ourselves between light cotton sheets on top of camping pads.

"Sarita?"

"Hmm?"

"Do you think people years and years ago—do you think they did the same thing?"

"What?" she asked sleepily.

"You know, making shadows on the walls?"

For a moment, I wasn't sure she'd heard me. Then she reached over and squeezed my hand. "I'm sure of it," she said. "That was fun! And I'm not even scared anymore."

"Me either. At least, not very much."

With the roar of water echoing all around us,

Caving

I tried to sleep. Instead of counting sheep, I fell asleep adding to my ever-growing list:

- ✶ *First time canoeing in a cave*
- ✶ *First time not being afraid of the dark*
- ✶ *First time making cave shadows*
- ✶ *First time camping in the belly of a giant*

8

Things That Go Bump in the Night

I woke to greenish-yellow light and water rush-rushing around me. Then I remembered. I'd slept on a sandbar—in a cave! I rolled over, and as I did, Sarita opened her eyes and smiled. "Hi," she said.

"Buenos dias," I said.

"Buenos dias—and a *good* day it is, too!"

We quickly threw on our clothes and stepped out. The cave wasn't nearly so scary in the morning hours. Beyond the dark ceiling, light filtered through a wall of intense green. I showed Sarita how to take down and pack up the tent, then grabbed the remains of the candle. I took one last look around. My shadow didn't tower on the cave wall any longer, but as I turned away, I some-how felt just a little bit taller.

"Hey, you survived!" Mr. Bol called as we climbed down the boulder-strewn path toward the campfire. He ladled scrambled eggs from a pan and pointed to the hot sauce. "Are you girls hungry? Breakfast is served."

As we were eating, the Cutwells zipped open their tent door. Mr. Cutwell's hair was wild and uncombed.

Things That Go Bump in the Night

Mrs. Cutwell looked as if she hadn't slept at all.

"Coffee," was all she said.

Mr. Bol poured hot water into a cup. "The instant coffee is right over there," he said. "And there's plenty of powdered milk, too."

Mrs. Cutwell groaned. "Instant coffee. Powdered milk. Well, what did I expect?"

Why *had* Mrs. Cutwell agreed to this trip? I imagined her at home in Texas, sipping an icy drink by a pool, book in hand. That seemed a truer picture.

Within the hour, we broke camp, packed up the Jeep, and headed off again.

"To reach the Xunantunich ruins," Mr. Bol explained, his arm draped over the wheel as always, "we'll have to take the ferry." When we reached the river, he drove onto a platform with pulleys, and we climbed out. Sarita and I stood near the man who operated the ferry, and I took photos.

The ferry operator cranked a large wheel, hand over hand, and moved us slowly across the green, swirling water. At the other shore, we drove on.

Towering white, with a central pyramid and smaller pyramids clustered around courtyards below, the Xunantunich ruins were much like the ones at Caracol. I had somehow expected them to be different.

"The Maya empire," Mr. Bol explained, leading the way as we climbed the ruins, "was a series of small kingdoms, each one directed by high priests and a royal family. Xunantunich was one such kingdom. It likely paid homage to the more powerful kingdom of its day, Tikal or Caracol." At the top of the largest pyramid, he explained that Maya high priests understood agriculture and astronomy and maintained calendars.

In the heat, I half-listened. The air was as thick as mashed potatoes. My shoulders reddened with sunburn, despite the sunscreen Sarita had slathered on them. And I hadn't refilled my water bottle from the jug in the Jeep. I squatted in the shade of a tower and rested. Around us, the jungle fanned out, seemingly forever, in a million shades of green and brown. It was the same as the area around Caracol, yet different in a way I couldn't explain.

After we climbed down, the Cutwells lingered in the buildings at the base of the ruins, where various Maya artifacts were displayed behind glass.

"Bob," Mrs. Cutwell said, motioning her husband to her side. "These jade pieces are amazin'. The artistry, the design of the jewelry, and that mask—it's just exquisite. They must date back to the Classic Period, maybe fifteen hundred years old. Darlin', just imagine!"

I could have told her that everything at ruin sites

was old, old, old. I tugged at Sarita's shirt hem and we moved back outside. We waited in the shade, watching a small lizard race upright across the ground. "Looks like he's in a hurry!" I said.

"Huh. Not like the Cutwells today."

"Mrs. Cutwell probably didn't sleep at all. I don't get why she thought this would be fun. She doesn't seem very interested in adventure. Only in artifacts."

"Me, either," Sarita said. "But I sure am glad they didn't mind our coming along. I wouldn't trade this for anything!" Her smile reached the corners of her eyes.

After we'd crossed the river again, Mr. Bol said, "Next on our schedule is a hike."

"A hike?" Mrs. Cutwell asked from the backseat. "Do you realize how hot it is today?"

Mr. Bol glanced back at her in the rearview mirror. "The jungle we'll be hiking through is so thick that we'll be lucky if we see daylight before we reach the top of the ridge. But if you'd rather stay back at the Jeep, that's certainly your choice. I don't want to push anyone beyond his or her limits."

Mrs. Cutwell flipped open another book and humphed. Her face was deep red, and a drop of sweat ran down her temple and the side of her face. I actually felt a little sorry for her.

The road narrowed and the jungle pressed closer around us. Mr. Bol stopped, seemingly in the middle of nowhere, and turned off the engine. "This is as far as the road goes." We hopped out as he grabbed his machete from the back. "Everybody have bug spray? Cameras? Water?" I made sure to refill my water bottle this time.

"Okay, then. Follow me." Mr. Bol led the way, with Mrs. Cutwell nearly stepping on his heels. Mr. Cutwell followed, and I was next, with Sarita trailing me. Even though she hadn't been caving before or gone on eco-adventures, Sarita did live in the jungle. Her dad had decided that she'd be less scared than I'd be at the back of the line.

Mr. Bol stopped along the way to point out butterflies. One sported brown spots on the sides of its folded wings, just like the eyes of an owl. "The owl butterfly," he said.

I clicked a photo. I could remember that one.

A large neon-blue butterfly flitted past through the undergrowth. "That's the Blue Morpho," Mr. Bol said. It was the most beautiful butterfly I'd ever seen. When it landed on a plant, I captured it with my camera. I couldn't wait to e-mail these photos to Heather.

Mr. Bol trekked on, hacking at vines and plants that threatened to overtake the thin trail. Now that the machete was being used, Mrs. Cutwell was keeping her distance.

At a mass of rounded, fragile bones, Mr. Bol stopped, silent. We clustered around.

"Well?" Mrs. Cutwell said. "Don't leave us hangin' in suspense. What is it?"

"A snake?" I asked.

"That's right, but what kind?" Mr. Bol said with a pleased smile.

Sarita knelt closer. "It was big. A boa constrictor?"

Mr. Bol now beamed, clearly proud of his daughter. "Exactly. Must have been over two meters."

I glanced at the mass of winding vines, branches, and leaves above and all around us. I knew there were snakes, but boa constrictors? Weren't they the ones that wrapped around their prey—animals, even people—and crushed them before swallowing them whole? I gulped. Did my parents have any idea how many dangerous things there were in the jungle? The machete suddenly made much more sense to me. No wonder children in the jungle were brought up to use one—and use it with skill.

Mr. Bol pointed ahead to the forest floor. I looked down but didn't see anything unusual, just a blanket of decaying leaves and twigs. "In the jungle, always watch where you're walking. Most snakes will want to get out of your path, but the most dangerous one, the *fer-de-lance,* blends in with the jungle floor and it won't move. It will attack you rather than get out of your way."

"I once almost stepped on a rattlesnake, but its rattling sound gave me a warning," I said. "Guess I'd rather get a warning."

The farther we hiked, the steeper the slope became. "If you slip, make sure that you don't grab the 'give and take' plant," Mr. Bol warned, pointing to a thick, thorny stem. "It will *give* you its thorns."

I joked, "And take your life?"

Mr. Bol didn't laugh in return. "Almost. Its thorns get into your body. If you should get a thorn, the way to treat it is with the same plant. So it *gives* you pain, but it also can *take* it away."

A few feet from the top of the slope, Mr. Bol put up his hand. "Move very slowly, very quietly now, and whatever you do, don't fall over the edge of the sink-hole. Not only is it a long drop to the trees below, but the floor of this cenote isn't filled with water. It's teeming with snakes."

I snatched Sarita's hand. If I was going to fall, it wasn't going to be alone! Just a few steps farther, the jungle opened to sky. We were standing on the edge of an immense, deep hole. It was bigger than a soccer field—

several soccer fields put together. Mr. Bol motioned for us to sit back from the edge.

Sarita and I braced our feet on a tree root and gazed out.

"Silence," Mr. Bol whispered, "is where wisdom lies. Besides, if you are quiet and still, you'll see more wildlife."

A breeze rustled through the treetops. Birds screeched and soared on air currents above the sinkhole. I spotted a number of birds on the distant rim, flying from tree to tree. I didn't say a word . . . I just watched. A few birds journeyed across the expanse, right to the trees above us. More slowly than a turtle, I turned my head and looked up.

The birds' big yellow beaks curved downward and their feathers were a mixture of black, yellow, and other bright colors. "Toucans!" I whispered. "Just like on Fruit Loops!"

"That's right, Miss Jess," Mr. Bol said under his breath. "Get your camera, but move slowly."

With the careful patience of a professional wildlife photographer, I slowly moved my camera from my pocket to my face, aiming, aiming, trying to find the birds amid the foliage. But before I could get a shot, they rose on air currents and circled away—above the sinkhole.

Mr. Bol turned to Mrs. Cutwell, who was sitting nearly in his lap. "Think for fun you'd like to rope-climb down? That's another optional eco-adventure I offer."

"Now that's a real good joke," she answered and actually laughed. Now that we were seated in one place, quiet and at ease, she seemed more relaxed.

For a long time, we watched toucans, falcons, and parrots fly in and around the cenote. Finally, Mr. Bol stood up, brushed off his khaki pants, and nodded toward the trail. "Let's find some lunch. Maybe there's a fast-food place around the next bend. What do you think, Miss Jess? What'll it be? Hamburger and fries? Chocolate shake?"

"Yum! Or sushi sounds good to me, too!" I laughed.

Back at the Jeep, Mr. Bol whipped up a meal. He handed each of us a plate of beans with rice and chicken. He used his machete to cut up fresh pineapple and papaya, and handed juicy slices all around. Everything was delicious.

"Michael," Mr. Cutwell said, sitting with Mrs. Cutwell on a mat on the side of the road, "this food is amazin'! You said you started it this morning—while we were sleeping?"

Mr. Bol looked up from his lunch and nodded, clearly pleased with their praise.

"Your dad's a great cook," I whispered to Sarita.

"Who knew? He only cooks when he's out guiding," Sarita whispered back. "At home, cooking is woman's work."

@

The last adventure of our day involved water, and lots of it. At the river's edge, Sarita and I took turns inflating kayaks with a foot pump. By the time we were finished, I was so hot, I thought I was going to pass out. But before I did, Mr. Bol instructed us to bring our kayaks down to the river's edge. "You're going to float and paddle for a few hours along a quiet stretch of the river. How does that sound?"

"Great!" I answered.

With only four kayaks, it was clear that Mr. Bol was not going to be joining us.

"Papa, aren't you coming?" Sarita asked anxiously.

He shook his head. "Somebody has to drive ahead to meet you. Unless you'd all like to hike back to the Jeep later. Might take two or three hours . . ."

Mrs. Cutwell waved him away. She seemed to have unexpected new energy. "No, you go ahead. The girls will do just fine with us. But how will we know where to get out?"

"You'll go under two bridges. Immediately after the second bridge, paddle hard to the right and I'll be there waiting. You can stop to swim at sandbars along the way."

I left my camera and pack in the Jeep and slathered on more sunscreen before putting on my life vest. Then I carried the featherweight kayak down to the river's edge. As Mr. Bol instructed, I rested the paddle across the middle of the kayak, then carefully climbed in. I wobbled at first but soon felt pretty comfortable. I tried the paddle—left, right, left—and set off. Mostly, the river did the work, carrying me downstream. I steered with my paddle, keeping the bow pointed straight ahead.

We floated under overhanging trees and wove around a random log or boulder. Water flowed gently over the sandy riverbed. Sarita and I paddled side by side. The Cutwells lagged behind, holding hands and floating kayak to kayak.

At one of the sandbars, Sarita motioned me to pull over. We took turns holding each other's kayaks and floated in the water to cool off. The water was knee-deep in some spots, over our heads in other places. Then we set off again.

Floating along, I kept a lookout for jaguars and tapirs. I saw neither, but I spotted a zillion iguanas.

"What about crocodiles?" Mrs. Cutwell called.

"My papa said they're upstream and downstream, but not here," Sarita called back. "But there are eels, turtles, and small piranha."

"Piranha?" Mrs. Cutwell cried, a nervous Nellie once again.

"Small ones. They might nibble, but that's all. Don't worry."

After that, I decided to stay in my kayak.

We passed beneath the first bridge, an old wooden one. Just beyond, a woman stood in the water, washing laundry. I waved to the woman and she waved back. Then I glanced at Sarita. "Easier than hauling water uphill?"

"Much easier!" she agreed.

Nearing the second bridge, the river seemed to be moving more swiftly. Beyond the bridge, on the right side of the river, Mr. Bol waved to us.

Sarita shot ahead, the water pushing her kayak back and forth. She screamed, but it sounded more like a scream of fun than of fear.

I followed behind her, trying to point my kayak toward the middle of the current, but the river pulled me off into an eddy and forced my kayak sideways. The limbs of a dead tree rose above the surface and caught my paddle. I didn't want to lose the paddle, and in the moment of clinging tight, my kayak twisted and snagged on the branches, dumping me into the river.

I screamed. "Sarita!" Instead of filling my lungs with air, I choked on water and went under. My life vest straps got tangled in the branches. I panicked. For a moment, I didn't know where up or down was. I opened my eyes to a swirl of brownish-green.

The kayak seemed everywhere at once—around me, on top of me, pushing with the full force of the river. I couldn't get away from it. My lungs burned, and I wanted to cry out. *Air! I need air! I need to get free!* Then, at the second I felt myself bursting open and about to inhale more water, I kicked as hard as I could and yanked myself free. Like a cork, I shot to the surface.

Untangled, my life vest now buoyed me up. I swam toward shore, toward Mr. Bol, who was plowing toward me through the shallows. His face told me that he was terrified he'd lost me. But he was only half as scared as I felt. He reached to scoop me up in his arms.

"The kayak," I said, coughing.

"Don't worry about the kayak."

He carried me to the shore. Mr. and Mrs. Cutwell pressed around me. Sarita was crying. "I couldn't see you," she cried. "You just disappeared!"

And then I started crying, too, even though I knew everything was okay. I'd almost drowned—and yet I hadn't. And as stupid as it seemed, while Sarita hugged me, her dad patted my back, and the Cutwells hovered nearby, I added to my list:

★ *First time kayaking*
★ *First time nearly drowning*

Some firsts, I vowed, never need to be repeated!

@

After Mr. Bol retrieved the kayak, we climbed into the Jeep and headed for home. Mrs. Cutwell kept glancing over at me, as if to make sure I was still breathing. She patted my hand—twice! After we dropped the Cutwells at their jungle lodge, Mr. Bol turned toward me in the backseat.

"Miss Jess," he said, his voice soft and fatherly. "With what you've been through today, I'd be happy to take you back tonight to your parents. Would you like that?"

The thought of Mom and Dad, and their arms around me, sounded good. I looked to Sarita, but her expression was one of waiting for me to decide, not of telling me what to do. We had planned to camp on top of the hill above her home. We were going to spend two more nights and days together. I didn't want to miss out on any of it.

I shook my head. "I'm ten," I said. "I'll be fine."

"You're sure?"

"Absolutely."

Sarita reached over and squeezed my hand. "Oh, good!"

9

Pippi's First Flight

The first thing we did was to check on Pippi inside the cook hut.

"She's always hungry," Mrs. Bol said. "Worse than little Luke."

Marcos and José stood near Pippi, who perched on the shoulder bag, which hung from a hook on the cook hut wall. She bobbed her head up and down at the boys. "Ack, ack!" she cried.

"We fed her and made sure she had fresh water," Marcos said proudly. "I'm teaching her to talk, too."

Sarita laughed. "I can tell!"

"What are you teaching her to say?" I asked. I reached toward Pippi to stroke the top of her head, but she nearly bit off my finger. I had to remember she was more wild than tame, and I hoped she always would be.

"I'm teaching her to say, um . . ."

Mrs. Bol turned from the corner, where she was stirring a pot. "Tell them, tell them, Marcos."

Marcos looked down at his bare feet, then glanced up, with a deepening dimple. "I . . . I've been teaching her to say, 'Marcos is smart.'"

Sarita didn't laugh. "Well, that's true. You are."
She turned to me. "Did I tell you that Marcos is the
smartest one in his class? He finishes his math problems
so fast that his teacher has to find extra work for him."

Marcos reddened, but he didn't deny it.

"Oh, that's wonderful," I said.

I enjoyed being around this family who lived
shoulder to shoulder and who seemed always to encourage
one another. I hadn't heard a mean or sharp word since I'd
met Sarita's family. They didn't have lots of things, or malls
to shop at, yet their lives were rich in ways I hadn't imagined
before. I loved my family, but we so often hurried here and
there, each doing his or her own thing—me racing to soccer
practice, Mom giving evening lectures at the college, Dad
working late in his study, Heather gone for weeks with play
practices, Jason working or at his friends' houses. Here,
everyone was together.

José tugged at my hand. "Want to see my schoolwork?" he asked shyly.

"Sure," I said, pleased to be asked.

From the metal cabinet in the corner, he pulled
out a folder, laid it on the wooden table, and leafed
through his drawings, one by one.

"Jaguar," he said, pointing to a paper with lots

of black marks in the center. If I looked closely, I could almost make out legs. Then he flipped through more sketches, explaining each one to me.

"This monkey is laughing. And this is a big toad. That ox is hungry," he explained seriously.

They were a little kid's drawings, but I felt good that he wanted to share them with me.

At a word from his mother, José cleared away his drawings, and Sarita and I set the table. Then we sat down for chicken-tortilla soup. I was suddenly so tired that I thought my head would fall into my bowl! But the hearty soup restored my energy, and as soon as we finished washing dishes, Sarita and I asked if we could set up the tent at the very top of the hill.

From the crest of the hill we could see for miles. A small fire pit and clearing were already set up for tenting. Sarita said that her parents often allowed tourists to camp there. Mr. Bol helped us haul our gear, but we put the tent up by ourselves. As we did, the sun dropped quickly and painted the sky in layers of orange, pink, and red.

We tied Pippi's shoulder bag to a loop inside our tent. She complained for a bit, but then she settled in her nest in the bottom of the bag and quieted down. I was so tired after our big day that I soon collapsed into a rock-hard sleep.

I woke to the soft song of mourning doves and the smell of smoke and something delicious. I turned over and found Sarita gone. So was Pippi. I unzipped the door, and several yards away, Sarita and her dad sat side by side on a log in front of a small fire. I reached back into the tent for my camera.

"Buenos dias," I said after I snapped a photo of the two of them.

"Good morning, Miss Jess!" Mr. Bol called. "Ready for breakfast?"

On the grate above the embers, a pan of scrambled eggs waited. "Help yourself. And there's tea, too. I thought you girls deserved some special treatment this morning before I took off." He stood. "Another day with the Cutwells. More ruins, more artifacts. You girls could come along, but maybe you'd rather be here today?"

Sarita nodded. "Let's stay, Jess."

After yesterday's kayak adventure, that sounded fine to me, so I nodded in agreement. As I sat on a log and ate breakfast, Mr. Bol hiked down toward the huts and his Jeep.

I glanced out at endless green, at wisps of smoke

rising above darkened patches, at farmlands stretching like multi-hued quilts. On a nearby tree, I noted Pippi's shoulder bag hanging from a broken branch, but something didn't look right. There wasn't a bulge at its base. It looked flat as a tortilla.

"Sarita! Where's Pippi?"

"Right there," she said, pointing to the bag. Then she jumped up. "She was there! She must have fallen—or flown? Do you think she could have flown? She's too young to fly, isn't she?"

"I don't know. She has a few feathers, even though they're scraggly. Maybe she flew, but I doubt she would have flown very far," I said.

Slowly, we turned in circles, carefully studying the ground around the stone fire pit, the branches of trees, the green leaves that could so easily be mistaken for a small green bird. Except that Pippi was brighter, a vivid and unmistakable green.

My heart and shoulders dropped. "What are we going to tell Barbara? I mean, she said Pippi was our responsibility!"

"We have to find her," Sarita said, grabbing my elbow. "She can't be far away. I'll go that direction—" she pointed toward the left. "You go that way," and she pointed to the right.

I shook my head. "No way. I'm not going into the jungle without you!"

"Pippi!" she called. "Pippi!"

I took up the call but doubted that a wild parrot, rescued only days before, would respond. Unless she was hungry. "Let's get a handful of pellets. Then if we find her, she might be persuaded to come close," I said. I grabbed the shoulder bag and put it across my chest. "And we'd better have this along, to be safe."

A small path wound down the back of the hill. "Let's go this way," Sarita said, motioning to me. Still in my pajamas, I followed behind her, wishing she had a machete in hand, in case we came across something dangerous. I pointed to what looked like an oversized football hanging from a branch overhead.

"What's that?" I asked.

"Just a termite ball."

"It's huge!" I hurried from underneath it.

Within a few yards, I stopped. Something bright caught my eye. I turned, and there, down the slope and deep in foliage, was Pippi, perched on a branch a foot above the ground.

"Oh, good!" I said, relieved. "Sarita, look. There she is!" I stepped off the trail, pushing branches and leaves aside as I walked. I forced myself to walk slowly.

I didn't want to scare her off, and I certainly didn't want to step on a snake.

"Ack! Ack!" Pippi fluttered her wings.

I gathered a few pellets in my hand and reached toward her. "Here you go, Pippi. You must be hungry."

Instead, Pippi jumped away, wings out, and coasted farther down the steep hillside, deeper into the jungle. For a moment I lost sight of her, then spotted her on top of a stump. She could manage short distances, but it was clear she wasn't able to take to the sky yet. All we could do was follow her.

"Remember, watch out for the poisonwood tree," Sarita called from behind. "There's one on your right."

Every time we drew closer and almost within reach, Pippi flitted away again, half hopping, half flying.

"This isn't a game!" I said to her. "You're bait out here. If you don't let us catch you, you'll be a meal for something!"

I started again after her, but my foot caught on a root, and I went tumbling. I was going to reach out to stop myself, but in the whir of my own limbs and the greenery, I remembered Sarita's warnings. Better to not grab anything. Instead, I let myself roll and fall until my shoulder stopped me against a rock.

"Oooooowwww!" I moaned. "Sarita!"

She scrambled down toward me. "Are you okay?" she called.

I moaned.

"Jess!?"

"I think I'm okay. I don't really know yet." At the base of the hill, I tried to focus. My vision blurred, then gradually became clear. Pippi perched just a few feet away. She opened her beak wide. "So now you think we should feed you, huh? Ouch!" I sat up slowly. The shoulder of my pajama top was ripped and my skin was scraped—almost bleeding, but not quite.

I stretched out my palm, with pellets still in hand. I couldn't believe I hadn't dropped them when I fell. This time, Pippi hopped closer and closer, then plucked the food from my hand.

Sarita also edged closer and clamped her hands around Pippi's fledgling feathers. Then she gently put our escapee in the shoulder bag, which was still strapped across my chest. "Good thing you didn't fall *after* we caught her," she said. "You would have crushed her."

I removed the shoulder bag and stood up. "Will you carry her?" I said. "I feel a little shaky. Really, I'm not always this klutzy."

As I brushed dirt and leaves from my pajamas, a crack in the ground caught my attention. There was a small hole beside the stone that I'd slammed into. Just seconds earlier, my head and shoulders had been right beside the dark hole. "Sarita," I said, pointing as I backed away. "Is that an animal's den? Or a snake's hole? What do you think it is?"

She leaned closer, hands to her knees. "When you fell, you must have moved that stone. See where the ground is scraped away?" She pointed.

"Think it's a home to anything—anything that might be dangerous?"

She shook her head. She grabbed a stick and started nudging away dirt and decayed leaves. I joined her, and soon it became clear that several limestone rocks formed a pile on either side of the hole. "It's as if some-one deliberately covered this up," Sarita said. "Covered up—I don't know—an entrance or something."

My heart sped up. Hadn't Mom said there were numerous Maya caves all across Belize? "Sarita, what if we've found a cave?" I picked up a small stone and dropped it into the dark crevice. One second, two sec-onds . . . then *plunk.* "We need to move this big stone," I said. "Then we'll know for sure."

A flat stone, twice the size of a laptop, was wedged into the dirt. Together we scraped away roots and soil, and then we pried with a larger stick at the rock's edge.

"Okay, one, two, three—push!" I said. The stone lifted, then toppled away.

A hole wider than my body dropped straight down into the earth. I peered in, then sat closer, dangling one leg toward the nearest knob of stone. Cool air rushed out. It invited me to climb in, to explore, to see what we'd discovered. Then I stopped myself. I didn't know how deep the hole went or if it was filled with water. This wasn't a time to rush ahead, to be foolish. I might find my way down, but that didn't mean I could climb back out again. I also realized that if it was indeed a sacred cave, we shouldn't move or disturb anything. I edged away and planted both my feet on solid ground.

"I think we'd better get your dad."

"He left to get the Cutwells, remember? But we can call him."

"Call him? You have a phone?"

She tilted her head as if I were crazy. "Of course, Jess," she said. "Everybody has a cell phone. We keep it in the cook hut."

10

Discovering the Past

We scrambled back up the tangled slope, this time with Pippi complaining but secure in the shoulder bag. At the top, I dove inside the tent, changed out of my pajamas, and jumped back out. "I'm ready! Let's hurry and call your dad before he's out of range."

The Bols kept their cell phone on top of the metal cupboard in the cook hut. I felt silly that I'd assumed the Bols didn't have a phone, but how was I to know that this was one modern convenience they did have? If I was learning anything since I'd arrived in Belize, it was to quit assuming I knew anything. While Sarita called her dad, I helped her mom carry water up the stairs.

"Papa," Sarita said into the phone, "I don't want to tell you. Just come—please! It's really important!"

Within a half hour, Sarita's dad pulled up with the Cutwells and hopped out of his Jeep. Sarita and I met them. "This is the Cutwells' tour day," Mr. Bol said. "Better be important, Sarita. Is someone hurt? Your mother? Little Luke?"

"No, Papa. We have to show you. But you'd better bring your climbing equipment."

He didn't move. "Climbing equipment."

"Please," I said, stepping forward. "It might be a huge discovery!"

At that, the Cutwells climbed out of the Jeep. "Well, I'm fixin' to find out what these girls are so worked up about, Michael," Mr. Cutwell said, sweeping his hair back with his hand. "Jus' might be fun."

Mr. Bol shook his head, then grabbed ropes and a backpack from the Jeep. "Okay, girls, lead on."

By the time we reached the top of the hill, we'd gathered the Cutwells, Mrs. Bol and the baby, and José and Marcos. I hoped that we hadn't imagined the entrance to be more than it was—just a hole in the ground.

"Follow me," Sarita said and waved everyone after her through the undergrowth and down the steep slope. "Watch your step. You don't want to tumble." She was just like her father—taking care of everyone.

"I can't believe," Mrs. Cutwell complained, but with a hint of humor in her voice, "that we're goin' on this wild-goose chase."

"It's here somewhere," Sarita said, stopping near the base of the hill, searching for the opening. "Honest, it is." She started veering to the left. "I'm sure it's this way."

I thought she might start crying.

Just slightly to the right I noticed a few broken branches—likely from where I'd plowed down the hill with my shoulder. And beyond by just a few steps lay the dark hole we'd uncovered.

I pointed. "There it is!"

Looking relieved, Sarita ran toward me. Everyone followed and gathered around the hole.

"This," Sarita said proudly, "is what we found."

Mr. Bol stared for a long time. His wife grabbed his arm. "We've owned this land for six years, Michael," she said quietly. "Why have we never found this before?"

I explained how I had fallen and how my shoulder had knocked the first stone away. I rubbed my sore shoulder, just to prove the point. Then we explained how Sarita and I had moved away more stones.

Mr. Bol moved away another stone, and the hole widened. Then, with a rope secured around his waist and the other end tied to a sturdy tree, he lowered himself down until we couldn't see him at all, not even his light.

"Michael," Mrs. Bol called down, holding the two older boys back from the edge. She carried Luke on her hip. "Be careful."

With an eerie echo, Mr. Bol's voice floated up. "You girls certainly found a cave! Not huge, but—"

"But what?" Mrs. Cutwell asked, hands on her knees, as if she was ready to dive in. She turned to Mrs. Bol. "Is he safe down there, Yollie? What if the air's bad?"

"I'm sure he knows what he's doing," Mr. Cutwell said confidently, sounding a bit like Mr. Bol.

Mr. Bol's voice grew more distant. "You won't believe it!"

Finally, he emerged into the light again and climbed out of the cave. He grinned broadly. "Now it's my turn to hold a secret."

"Papa—you can't," Sarita groaned. "Tell us!"

He shook his head. Then, swiftly, he swung his machete and cut two long wooden poles from the jungle around us. Everyone watched as he cut notches and then strapped wooden steps to the poles with short lengths of twine. Before long, he'd crafted a simple ladder.

"It's not that deep," he said, lowering the ladder into the hole. "I'll go first. Then you can all come down—but only two at a time. Sarita and Jess—you two should come first."

I climbed down into the darkness, breathing damp, ancient air. My insides tickled with fear, with excitement, with an I-can't-believe-this-is-happening feeling. When my feet struck bottom, I reached for Sarita's hand. The cave was alive, drip-dripping all around us. I turned on my

My insides tickled with an I-can't-believe-this-is-happening feeling.

flashlight, but Mr. Bol's headlamp shone directly into my eyes, and so for a few seconds I couldn't see a thing.

"Move slowly," he warned, "and watch your head." Then he shone the light around. The cave was as big as the belly of a whale—not nearly as big as Rio Frio Cave or Barton Creek Cave, but big enough! Our lights swept up and around, toward the ceiling, past hanging stalactites and towering stalagmites to hundreds of artifacts!

There were pots bigger than I could reach my arms around. Lots of them. I knew that the pots would have been used to collect the pure water that dripped into the cave. Drinking cups, knives, mallets, pounding stones, and smaller bowls were clustered together on ledges and on the cave's uneven floor. Many objects were broken, yet just as many were intact.

"Girls," he whispered. "This cave was last used by the ancient Mayas. Think of it. Water bowls, ceremonial bowls . . . it's all here, just as they left it hundreds and hundreds of years ago."

I shivered. I expected colorfully dressed Mayas with sloping foreheads to step from the shadows.

We followed Mr. Bol deeper into the cave. "Girls, look," he said, and his light swooped along a row of spearheads, hatchet heads, and seashells—until finally, the light stopped on two skeletons.

Sarita gasped. I jumped, nearly tripping into a set of bowls to my side.

Two human skeletons rested side by side. We were stunned into silence.

A distant voice called to us. "Are you okay down there?" It was Mrs. Cutwell.

"We're fine!" Mr. Bol called back, then turned back and pointed at the skulls. "Look, they must have been a stylish pair. Their teeth are inlaid with jadeite and pyrite for decoration."

"Oh yeah," I said. "My mom explained to me how they did that. They chewed on allspice leaves to numb their mouths before fitting the stones into their teeth."

Mr. Bol nodded. "That's right, Miss Jess. And see the other objects around them? Meant to accompany them into the underworld, into the afterlife. The Mayas performed human sacrifices, believing there was no greater sacrifice to make."

I glanced around, trying not to imagine this place being used for anything other than feasting. But I knew better. I'd heard and read about how the Mayas sacrificed humans, believing that it was a great honor and that it pleased their gods. In that way, their world was hard for me to understand.

But Mr. Bol continued, "They believed that when people died, their spirits were first greeted in the underworld. This cave would have been thought of as something like a gateway to the underworld—and eventually their spirits would circle up to the heavens."

I shuddered. To step into a cave that had never been explored by scientists or tourists, to find a cave that had been waiting for hundreds and hundreds of years—it was all too much for my brain to take in. A cave where real human beings had sacrificed their lives! It was strange—almost unthinkable. But for the first time, I understood why my parents loved their work. It was all about discovery and mystery. About finding something unusual and awe-inspiring from a distant time and imagining what had been. *Who were these people? Why had they been chosen to give their lives?*

I pulled my camera from my pocket and took pictures of everything. The flash reflected off the cave walls. I couldn't wait to show my parents the photos and e-mail them to my class and to Heather and Jason. As I was photographing all of the artifacts and the two skeletons, I noticed a pile of rocks the size of cantaloupes wedged into a corner of the cave.

"Sarita," I said. "Mr. Bol, look over there. See those rocks piled against that corner?"

"I don't see anything unusual," said Mr. Bol.

"I know, but I'm thinking that if early Mayas hid their tombs and entrances as well as they could—"

"Like this cave, right?" said Sarita, stretching her arms wide. "Otherwise this all would have been found long ago."

"Right. And that pile might be hiding something else. See how those stones are heaped up? It looks deliberate," I said, "but maybe it's nothing."

"But maybe it's *something*, too," Sarita said. "We found the cave, right?'

Mr. Bol shined his headlamp at the corner. I moved closer. The stones covered another hole!

Sarita squatted closer, shining her flashlight and peering in. "Jess, you were right! I think we can crawl in."

"It's yours to explore," Mr. Bol said. He removed his headlamp and handed it to me. "Jess? If you think you can fit through without disturbing anything, go ahead and try."

"Really?" I hesitated, unsure about it.

"It's been sealed up, so you needn't worry about spiders or snakes."

I mustered up my courage and, with both the headlamp and my flashlight, started crawling. I had to inch in on my belly and elbows. Sarita was right behind me, and I appreciated it when she touched my ankles.

"I'm right behind you," she said.

"Thanks," I whispered. "I wouldn't want to do this alone."

"That's for sure," Sarita said. "And guess what—you don't have to whisper."

"I know," I whispered.

We crawled in about three body lengths, and my light flickered upward. Carefully, I emerged from the tunnel into a room—a cave big enough to stand in. "Oh, wow!" I whispered. "It's a storeroom!"

Sarita scrambled the rest of the way in and stood up next to me. Her mouth froze open.

Against one wall, ledges overflowed with pots of all sizes and countless other artifacts. Neither of us touched anything. We just stood side by side in the amber glow of the storeroom, between light and shadow, between past and present. I couldn't believe it. I'd followed an inkling and a little knowledge—and look what we'd discovered.

After a few minutes, we turned around and crawled out of the tunnel.

"Well?" Mr. Bol asked. "What did you find?"

Sarita smiled. "It's a secret. You'd better go in and see for yourself."

The Cutwells never got back on schedule that afternoon. But they didn't seem to mind, once they climbed down into the cave themselves. "Well, I'll be jiggered," Mr. Cutwell said, wiping sweat from his forehead and the back of his neck when he climbed back up. "Here we were fixin' to go see more ruins and artifacts, and you girls found your very own sacred cave!"

Mrs. Cutwell's voice lifted with genuine enthusiasm. "Just amazin'! You girls are unbelievable!"

Mr. Bol notified the people at the Institute of Archaeology in Belize City, who promised to send out a research team within the next few days. "In the meantime," he explained to us by the entrance, "we're of course not to touch or move any of the artifacts." His eyes rested an extra moment on José. "And that goes for you, too."

To celebrate, Mrs. Bol grilled some chicken over the fire pit at the top of the hill that evening. We all sat around on logs, talking, eating, and tossing chicken bones into the embers. The boys ran around the edge of the firelight. Sarita and I took turns holding Luke.

"To be safe," Mr. Bol said, "first thing tomorrow morning, I'm going to build a sturdy grate over the cave's entrance. I'll anchor it in cement and then lock it."

His wife nodded agreement. "Word spreads quickly around here," she said.

Mr. Bol's face was radiant by the firelight. "I'm thinking that we can open it up for tours, tell people about how this cave was discovered by our girls." He winked in our direction. "And the way I see it, if we take good care of the cave, it will take care of us, too."

As the moon climbed higher and cast a bright white glow over the hilltop and valley below, Mr. and Mrs. Cutwell stood up, holding hands. "Well, Michael, this has been grand, but can we get a lift back to the lodge?" asked Mr. Cutwell.

Mr. Bol laughed and tipped an imaginary hat to them. "You aren't likely to catch a taxi out this way now, are you?"

After everyone left, Sarita and I climbed into the tent. Under the sheet, I rested on my elbows and stared out the screen door. We had doused the fire with a bucket of water, but a few stubborn coals flickered red. All around us, cicadas sang. Pippi rustled around in her nest, then settled quietly.

"Just think," I whispered. "We're sleeping almost right above the cave."

"I know," Sarita said. *"Our* cave."

Discovering the Past

As I drifted off to sleep, I made a mental addition to my long list of firsts:

★ *First archeological discovery*

11

Digging Deeper

That night, I dreamed about the cave. I was exploring deeper and deeper and not able to find my way out, discovering an aqua-green river, then getting swept by its current deeper into the cave, only to come face-to-face with ancient Mayas. Their bodies were painted in bright colors and several spoke to me, but as hard as I tried, I couldn't understand their words.

Their voices woke me.

I sat upright.

"Sarita," I whispered. "Did you hear that?"

She turned and rose on her elbow. "What?"

"Voices."

"Probably ghosts," she said dreamily. "We're sleeping near a burial site. You must've been dreaming."

"Oh, great." I lay down again.

Howler monkeys began to roar and bellow in distant treetops.

"Jess, remember, they only *sound* dangerous."

With each breath, I became more awake. What if I really had heard voices nearby? "I'm going to turn on the flashlight and see what—"

I flicked on the light. Pippi emerged from the shoulder bag. "Ack! Ack!"

"Shh," I said. "It's not morning yet, Pippi. Go back to sleep."

I unzipped the tent but didn't dare step out. In slow motion, I shined the light across the hilltop. No embers glowed in the fire pit. The light caught something moving. I moved the flashlight back. A toad hopped.

"What do you see?" Sarita asked, her hand clamped tightly on my arm.

"Just a big toad."

When the howler monkeys stopped their clamor, I heard voices again—the deep voices of men, and coming from somewhere beyond our tent.

"Sarita!" I whispered, my heart jumping to my throat.

She bolted upright. "I heard them."

"From that way, right?" I pointed in the direction of the cave.

She nodded.

I trembled and suddenly wished I were back at the dig site with my parents. "Who would be wandering around out here in the middle of the night?" I whispered into Sarita's ear. "I'm scared."

"Me, too."

I turned off my flashlight and tucked myself deeper under the flimsy sheet. "Sarita?" I said, my tongue nearly stuck to the roof of my mouth. "What if it's someone trying to steal from the cave? Looters? We have to let your dad know—"

"But if we get out of the tent, and they see us—" she began.

"But we can't just let someone steal from our cave!"

We quickly slipped on our sandals, slowly and quietly unzipped the tent door, and then held hands as we made our way in the dark down the opposite slope to the Bol family's hut.

◎

Within seconds of our knocking on the door and explaining in a rush why we were there, Mr. Bol was armed, machete in hand. "You girls stay here," he said, the blade glinting.

"But Papa," Sarita cried. "You could get hurt!"

"If we wait until the authorities get here, it will be too late."

In her nightgown, Mrs. Bol shook her head at us. "You're staying here until he returns." When Sarita's father stepped outside, Mrs. Bol bolted the door with a thud. "Now, you two go lie down until he returns."

Sarita and I squeezed side by side into the hammock in the corner. "Perhaps it would have been better if we'd never found the cave," I whispered, trying not to wake her little brothers. "If we hadn't found it, your dad wouldn't be out there now in the middle of the night."

Minutes passed like hours. I drifted in and out of sleep and worry.

What if this turned deadly? If Mr. Bol ran into thieves, would they fight back? If he got hurt, then what good was there in finding the cave? His safety was more important than any archeological discovery.

When we heard a quiet knock, Sarita and I both tumbled out of the hammock.

"Michael?" Mrs. Bol asked. She opened the door.

"It *was* looters," Mr. Bol said heavily, stepping in with his machete hanging at his side. "You girls were right."

"How much did they steal?" I asked. "Did they get everything?"

"Lots of smaller items. They left the largest pots. Soon as they heard me holler, they scrambled out of the hole. I was on the hill, carrying extra flashlights to make it look like there were more on my side. They took off."

"Did they find the tunnel?" Sarita asked.

He shook his head. "If you girls hadn't been so brave and let me know, they would have emptied the whole cave. Of that I have no doubt."

I was relieved that Mr. Bol had returned safely, but now I was sick for another reason. If we'd never found the cave, then everything in the burial site would have been untouched for many more years to come.

Mr. Bol paced, talking more to himself than to anyone else. "Doesn't make sense that word could have spread so quickly . . . "

"Girls," Mrs. Bol said, "it's four in the morning. You sleep here for the rest of the night."

We didn't argue, and though my mind whirred, I fell asleep in the hammock beside Sarita, feeling safe in the hut with her family.

When we woke up, the sun glared high in the sky. "Pippi!" I said. "We forgot her in the tent. She'll be going crazy by now!"

I rolled out of the hammock and sent Sarita in a heap to the floor. "Oh, I'm sorry. I didn't mean to do that!"

She blinked. "It's okay. I'm wide awake now." I held out my hand and helped her to her feet.

In the tent, Pippi was squawking her head off.

She was walking around and making a mess all over our bedding. "More wash to do," Sarita said with a grin. We took turns feeding Pippi. When she finished taking pellets from our hands, she preened her feathers with her beak.

"You look lovely," I told her, then grabbed the shoulder bag from its loop. I held it beside Pippi's feet and she stepped onto the edge. I eased her small body inside with a nudge and shut the top. Then I put the bag over my shoulder.

Breakfast waited for us on the table in the cook hut. Sarita's mom turned from the oven, where something delicious was baking. "Your eggs are cold, but they're still good."

"Where's Papa?" Sarita asked as she sat down.

"He's been up for hours putting a grate on the entrance to the cave. He already went to get the Cutwells. Needs to get them to the airport."

"I wouldn't think they'd take the bus," I said with a grin, remembering my sweltering ride from Belize City. Mrs. Cutwell would simply wilt and die before she reached her destination.

After lunch, a park vehicle pulled up at the base of the hill. Mom, Dad, and Barbara climbed out and trekked up to the cook hut—all smiles.

"We heard about your discovery," Dad called. "Michael phoned us last night."

I ran to him, and he lifted me off the ground and twirled me around. I was thrilled to see them! I had so much to tell them.

"So, you girls found a cave, is that right?" Mom asked, planting a kiss on the top of my head.

"You won't believe it," I said, leading them and Barbara to the cook hut, where Mrs. Bol waited in the doorway with Sarita at her side. "The *good* news is we found a cave—" I started.

Sarita broke in. "But looters. That's the bad news," she said. "They stole from the cave last night!"

The smiles quickly faded. My parents' faces looked as pained as if someone had died. "That's terrible!" Mom said. "How?"

Dad removed his cap and put it back on several times, as if doing so might change the facts. "When?"

And Barbara said, "How could word have possibly spread that fast?"

"But we stopped them," I said. "I mean, Mr. Bol stopped them before they could take everything. Do you want to see what's still there?"

Mrs. Bol held out a key on an orange ribbon. She put it over Sarita's head. "This is for the new grate," she said. "Don't lose it."

We grabbed some flashlights, and Sarita and I guided Mom, Dad, and Barbara to the other side of the hill. The steel grate had two locks on each side. Sarita opened them and put the orange ribbon back around her neck. Then Dad helped us move the grate aside. The cement was already hard.

"My papa built a ladder," Sarita said, pointing. "Watch your step and watch your head."

Inside the cave, I felt like a tour guide explaining how we found the site. I swept my flashlight across the cave's interior, and even in the dim light I saw that Mom's and Dad's faces were lit up like those of little kids at a parade. But I saw that what Mr. Bol had said was true. Where there had been clusters of artifacts, only empty spaces remained. The thieves had taken the smaller objects—spearheads, small bowls, necklaces. If Mr. Bol hadn't scared them off, they would have emptied the cave completely.

"To think you stumbled upon this!" Dad said.

My shoulders sagged. "But yesterday, there was even more."

"Still," Mom said, "it's quite a find."

"Luckily, I took photos of everything first. And they didn't find this," I said, pointing to the small opening in the corner. "The tunnel to the storeroom." Mom and Dad eagerly crawled in to explore.

While we waited in the main part of the cave, Barbara said, "You must have had good teachers to find this tunnel, Jess."

"The best," I said, realizing for the first time how much I'd picked up from my parents over the years. And for the first time, I was honestly grateful that they loved their work enough to share it with me—and that they'd allowed me to come with them to Belize.

Several minutes later, Mom and Dad emerged from the tunnel, their faces and hands smudged with dirt.

"You're true archeologists!" Mom said, wrapping her arms around my shoulders and Sarita's.

"Good work, girls," Dad said. "You've found an amazing wealth of artifacts. And you stopped the looters by alerting Sarita's dad. Otherwise they'd have gotten their hands on every last item and sold it on the black market. What you did took courage and quick thinking."

When we returned to the house, Mr. and Mrs. Bol were visiting with the Cutwells under the shade of the awning. Mr. Cutwell called to us and said, "We couldn't leave without sayin' good-bye to y'all!"

"And without apologizin'," Mrs. Cutwell added in a wavery voice. "We heard the terrible news." With her arms crossed tightly around her waist and her head bowed, she began again. "Looters disturbed your cave last night. And it's all my fault!"

"But Mrs. Cutwell, how could it be your fault? When Sarita and I were in the tent, we heard—"

But Mrs. Cutwell held up her hand, clearly not wanting to have her apology interrupted. "When we returned to the lodge last night, I was so excited about your discovery that I'm afraid I may have talked too much. We sat down and had a few drinks with other guests at the lodge, as well as with some of the staff. Without thinking, I must have given all the details someone needed to find and steal from the cave." Tears pooled in her eyes. Her chin and nose puckered. "I'm so darned sorry."

Now I understood, and my stomach sank. A few casual words by Mrs. Cutwell had put the artifacts at risk. I recalled what Mom and Dad had said about looters on our flight into Belize. Their worries hadn't seemed too real to me then.

Mr. Bol put his arm across Mrs. Cutwell's back. "Word would have spread fast even if you hadn't said anything. Don't be too hard on yourself, Marianne.

Besides, we have a saying: 'When it rains, it rains on everyone's hut, not just on one.'"

"Seein' that cave with y'all," she went on, crying through her words, "was life-changin' for me. One of the highlights of my life. I just want you to know I never intended any harm. And you girls have been so sweet—"

I wanted to be angry, but how could I? I actually felt so bad for Mrs. Cutwell that I jumped up and gave her a hug, and then Sarita did the same. Of course, then Marcos and José were right behind, until Mrs. Cutwell nearly toppled from so much hugging. Her eyes were red and puffy from crying, but she was smiling at the same time.

Who would have guessed? It was true what they said about Belize: *Expect the unexpected.*

After Sarita's mom served us sweet buns and lime juice, everyone said good-bye. The Cutwells waved from their windows as the Jeep disappeared down the dirt road to the airport in Belize City.

It was time for me to gather my things and leave Sarita's home. As I put my hand on the wood railing, ready to take the steps down to Barbara's park service truck, Mom turned to Mrs. Bol. "I know this might seem excessive," she said, "but could Sarita return to Caracol with us for one more day?"

What was Mom up to? I stopped, waiting to see in which direction this sudden breeze was going to blow.

"I think they've had plenty of time together—" Mrs. Bol started to say, rocking Luke in the hammock. Mom stepped closer and spoke quietly.

Mrs. Bol nodded slowly. "Oh, that's different. I see."

Sarita waited near her mother. "Mama, may I?"

"You'll have an extra day's wash to do when you return," she said.

Sarita smiled and did a quick twirl in the dirt.

"Yes!" I exclaimed.

"And Jess," Mom said to me, "after tomorrow, you'll need to get focused again on your schoolwork. You can't afford to get behind."

I didn't know why Mom was doing this, but I wasn't about to complain.

My parents insisted that Sarita and I ride up front with Barbara, and with our seat belts buckled tight. I kept glancing back at them in the truck bed. They leaned into one another, holding hands, their hair blowing in the hot, dusty wind. They didn't seem to mind a bit.

That evening we ate inside Café Cabana instead of under the stars. People kept coming by to congratulate us on our discovery. Mom said, "We're having a special gathering tonight after dinner, so you and Sarita should come straight to the bonfire, okay?"

"Sure." How could I say no when she'd been nice enough to let Sarita and me have more time together? After we took care of Pippi's evening feeding, we left her safely behind on a perch we'd rigged in the hut. Though she was full, she still complained, wanting our attention. "Ack, ack, ack!"

Halfway through the screen door, I turned back, feeling just like a parent. "Don't worry," I said. "We'll be back before you know it."

As Sarita and I crossed the field and headed toward the bonfire at the center of camp, I swept my flashlight beam back and forth. I didn't want to step on the fire ant highway again. Once was enough.

The air was rich with the damp, earthy smells of the jungle. We walked closer to the bonfire as it sent a stream of red glitter into the night sky. I glanced up at the countless stars, not spotting anything familiar. No Big Dipper or Orion's Belt or Milky Way. I was so far

from home that even the constellations were different.
I wished Heather and Jason could be here now. I had
so much I wanted to tell them.

Dozens of people from the dig—some of the
college students, professors, volunteers, and even
the Café Cabana staff—were gathered around the fire.
In its glow, the ruins towered faintly beyond. As we
neared the group, Dad stepped forward with his guitar
strapped across his chest.

"Cheers! Congratulations to Sarita and Jess, our
two budding archeologists!" He began clapping and
everyone else joined in.

"Surprise! Hooray!" They all shouted and cheered
and whistled.

"A party?" I asked.

Sarita laughed and squeezed my arm. "For us?"

A week earlier, I couldn't have imagined any of
this—a new friend, adventures, a big discovery, or this
celebration. Now so much had changed. I'd changed! Not
so much in days and weeks—or in how many miles I was
away from home—but in the way I saw things and the way
I saw myself. I would always be the youngest in my family,
but I could never be the baby of the family again.

Uncomfortable with all the attention, yet loving
every second of it, I stood in front of the group, touching

shoulders with Sarita. Everyone—Mom, Dad, and many familiar faces—cheered for us. Someone started singing a local folk song and Dad joined in on his guitar.

When they finished, Barbara stepped forward, with Fuzz chattering beside her. "Girls, everyone's eager to hear about your amazing discovery!"

Sarita and I glanced at each other. I'm sure my smile was as big and proud as hers. Before either of us spoke a word, I silently added to my list:

✴ *First time sharing my own story at a dig!*

Meet the Author

Mary Casanova loves to travel to research her books. To write *Jess*, she explored the jungles of Belize in Central America. "Nearly everything Jess experiences, I did, too–including being attacked by fire ants." She believes in making life an adventure, whether at home or away. She and her husband live in northern Minnesota, where they ride their horses, Lexi and JJ, and kayak with their dogs, Kito and Chester.